DAVID A. ESTES

BYE BYE, Sweet Susie

Cover Design: Sharon Kizziah-Holmes

Paperback-Press
an imprint of A & S Publishing
A & S Holmes, Inc.

.

ISBN-10:1-945669-28-4
ISBN-13:978-1-945669-28-6

i

CHAPTER 1

Who is Susie McCord?

Whoa! Did that billboard really say that?

On the blacktop outside the Marlow city limits, Jeff Timberlake skidded his red Corvette to a stop and scooted back for another look.

The yellow-on-black sign screamed at him: SUSIE McCORD DIED HERE!

Hmmnn.

He eased the Corvette forward, pondering who Susie McCord was, when she died, and why? His nose itched with curiosity. He guessed she was somebody important, else why would anyone want the world to know she died there? Interesting. Or, as Charlie Chan might say: Velly intelesting.

Jeff's instincts told him there was a story behind that sign, prodding him to find out what it was. He couldn't shake the notion that all was not sweetness and light in the city of Marlow, Missouri. At the moment, however, his gurgling stomach cried out for nourishment. He turned left onto Main Street in search of a restaurant to ease its pain, puzzled by the ominous message of the Susie sign.

On the seat beside him lay the white envelope his mother pressed into his hand with her dying breath. Curiosity pushed him to open it, but Jeff resisted the temptation to break the seal and look inside. It belonged to Zachary Wheeler. In a town as small as Marlow, Jeff guessed, Wheeler shouldn't be hard to find. That done, he'd move on to St. Louis and check on a radio news job he heard about. He wouldn't have to do that if Fat Marvin hadn't kicked him off the air in Des Moines.

Jeff winced at the recollection as he pulled into a parking spot in front of the first eating place he saw—Dottie's Diner on the southwest corner of the Marlow square.

In most small Missouri towns the "square" was the hub of activity. Whittlers and spitters congregated on the wooden benches anchored by metal bolts to the concrete sidewalk surrounding City Hall. The Hall occupied a major portion of the square. It was a gathering place for farmers who sat elbow-to-elbow on wooden benches and complained about the low market price for hogs, or to brag about how many bushels of corn they got to the acre.

A favorite topic, of course, was politics. They agreed that Ike was doing a good job in the White House, but they got frothy at the mouth because nobody passed laws to "keep them damn

Democrats" out of Congress!

"Them damn Democrats," somebody piped up, passed the laws that kept them in office.

On holidays and other special occasions the townsfolk covered the wooden picnic tables with red-and-white checkered cloths. They shared with their neighbors' fried chicken, pork chops, sweet potatoes and banana pudding. From hand-cranked freezers some kid sat on to keep it steady, a washtub of homemade ice cream didn't last long.

Brass bands from area schools performed on the raised wooden platform.

Politicians expounded on Memorial Day and the Fourth of July, paying tribute to "our heroes who gave their lives so we could stand up here and talk about it."

Independence Day fireworks attracted people from miles around. Some brought blankets for a stay when there was a revival meeting going on in the big tent on the edge of town.

Marlow was home to 793 souls, not counting the ones who moved away but still called Marlow "home." Those who migrated to other parts of the state came back for Mother's Day, Christmas, family birthdays and anniversaries.

Marlow was a close-knit town where most of the residents were born. "When one of us itches," they said, "we all commence to scratch."

Many of them owed their livelihood to Amos Marlow whose grandfather Silas established the town a hundred years before. Amos's father Eli followed in his footsteps and plastered the Marlow name on everything worth owning, including the bank, the grain elevator, and the lumber mill with the town's biggest payroll.

Amos also owned a few people. One of them was Chink Petty, the local deputy sheriff. From the day Chink pinned that brass badge above the left pocket of his khaki shirt, Amos paid his salary. That was eight years ago.

City Hall was an ancient gray stone structure whose tower housed a huge clock with gold-plated hands sweeping a background of white Roman numerals. Every hour on the hour the clock blared the strains of "Oh, What a Beautiful Morning". Some local citizens derided the clock as a public nuisance. The ACLU declared it a "culture medium," and as such the clock was an expression of free speech. The ACLU was not highly regarded as a spreader of the gospel, but nobody dared challenge the call.

At one o'clock on a sunny Thursday afternoon in September, 1958, the clock rendered its version of the classic from the Rogers and Hammerstein long-running Broadway musical "Oklahoma!" The city fathers decided the stirring melody would be a wonderful tribute to the composers. They were invited to attend the unveiling of the clock twelve years before.

Rick and Ossie, however, begged to be excused because they would be "out of town" the day of the dedication.

Timberlake jumped like he was shot at the sound of the clock's shattering blast. He threw up an arm to protect himself from the blaring onslaught, and pushed open the glass door to Dottie's Diner.

***

Saying goodbye to the house where he was born thirty-two years before wasn't easy. But, for Jeff Timberlake, life had never been easy.

The loss of his mother added to the load of sadness his life style hadn't prepared him to carry. From where he stood in the middle of the front room, he knew his mother would expect him to look back on the past, and stash away a head full of precious memories to carry with him to wherever the future took him.

He couldn't do that without dredging up the unhappy times of his childhood. Recalling his father's scriptural harangues, to which he and his mother Leota were subjected, Jeff still felt chills shooting down his spine. His father was a fundamentalist preacher. His "holier than thou" pronouncements he didn't reserve for the pulpit. He thrust them upon his wife and son with irritating frequency.

Five years ago, Jeff's mother called him with the news that his father "passed." Jeff could not cry. He felt nothing, except sorrow that he felt nothing. A man should feel something—remorse —sadness—joy?—when his father dies.

Jeff slipped a hand into a pocket for the brass key that would lock the front door when he closed it for the last time. Out with the key came the small white envelope his mother pressed into his hand on her death bed. He read again the words scrawled across its face: Zachary Wheeler, 311 Oak Street,

Marlow, Missouri.

Jeff didn't know Zachary Wheeler. He pondered why his mother's last words were, "Tell Zack about me." If it meant that much to her, however, he would honor her dying wish and deliver the envelope to the mysterious Zack Wheeler.

Never again would he see the house where he spent the first eighteen years of his life.

Sun-streaked cotton curtains still covered the front window where the brown camelback sofa slumped beneath it. He hated the stark white walls last painted when he was nine. The faded green carpet's frazzled path extended from the front door to the kitchen. Against a wall of the living room stood the ancient pump organ his mother cherished. On the lamp table beside the sofa lay the King James Version of the Holy Bible. Opened to the 29th chapter of Proverbs his father read for the last time. The margins of its yellowed pages were cluttered with penciled notations.

The verse that caught Jeff's eye was number three: "He who loves wisdom makes his father glad, but one who keeps company with harlots squanders his substance."

He closed the Bible and turned to go. He would leave behind anything that reminded him of the past.

Jeff took a last look around then closed the front door behind him. He locked it, and tossed the brass key into a zinnia bed at the end of the concrete porch. Neither of them he would see again.

A gentle breeze ruffled his sandy hair as he headed for the red Corvette parked at the curb. He settled behind the wheel, started the motor, and pointed it south toward Missouri.

He never looked back.

CHAPTER 2

The Red Car Comes to Town

Mason Bryer was one of the "foreign born" who settled in Marlow. He took early retirement from the IRS and trooped all the way from Whittier, California to escape big city crime, he said, and life threatening traffic, and what he called the "cold impersonality of uncaring people."

To separate himself from such unpleasantness, Mason moved to quiet, countrified Marlow, Missouri. He bought the local newspaper, "The Marlow Voice", with plans for making it the vital organ of community reform.

He learned early the Marlowites didn't want to be reformed. They liked things the way they were, the way they had always been. Foiled in his noble mission to reform the reluctant populace, Mason was forced to confine his editorial prowess to waging campaigns condemning the dirty words scrawled on the city sidewalks, and painting the water tower red on Halloween. Mason hated that. Most of all, Mason hated Amos Marlow.

The top of Mason's scarred wooden desk was littered with newspapers, magazines, and artwork catalogs. An ancient Remington typewriter peeked out from under the rubble. He scowled at the phone in his beefy hand, not pleased with what was coming out of it and entering his elephantine hearing organ.

Mason thumbed his reading glasses onto his broad, freckled forehead, and swiveled around in his chair, waving his impatient hand, waiting for an opening to spout his agitated rejoinder. His fuse was about to explode. The caller paused for breath, and Mason leaped in.

"People don't give a hoot in hell about that stuff, Congressman," Mason bellowed into the phone. "You don't know shit from Shinola about what people want. If you'd spend some time here in your home district, you'd know what's going on around here."

Mason's flabby jowls were red with rage. On the verge of hanging up on the caller, he glanced out his office window overlooking the square.

He spotted a red car easing along Main Street, and bounced to his feet. Leaning toward the window for a better look, he squinted to be sure his eyes weren't deceiving him. The red Corvette pulled into a parking spot in front of Dottie's Diner.

Waving an arm in a windmill motion, into the phone he shouted, "Call me back sometime,

Congressman, when you've got something I can use!"

He slammed the phone down and yelled, "Sally!"

Hello, Dottie

Against the left wall of Dottie's Diner sat three tables with four chairs each. The counter stretched along the right side of the narrow room. The counter was lined with seven round, red leather-covered stools. The cash register was mounted on the end of the counter nearest the door. From the jukebox beside the entrance, Elvis shouted, "You ain't nothin' but a hound dog!"

Jeff slid onto one of the red stools at the counter. His nostrils were attacked by the pungent odor of frying burgers, fries and onions from the serving window behind the counter. He reached for the plastic-covered menu tucked between the paper napkin holder and the sugar dispenser with the hole in the top. Checking the menu, Jeff felt upon him the eyes of a tall, buxom woman behind the counter, soaking up coffee drippings from the countertop with a white towel. Big boned and green eyed, she was, with gray-streaked brown hair piled on top of her head.

She tossed the towel under the counter, and wiped her hands on her food stained, formerly white apron. To the young man perusing her menu, she said, "Now, what can I do you for, hon?"

"Am I too late for breakfast?" Jeff said.

"Hell no! We serve breakfast all day long. If you

want breakfast, you get breakfast."

"How about this stack of wheat cakes?"

She lowered her head and scrutinized him from the tops of her eyes. "If you want enough wheat cakes to last you for about three days," she said, "you order that stack. But, if you're just looking for something to tide you over till supper time, you better go with the short one. It lops over the sides of the plate and runs half way down to the river. By the time you wrap your gums around that, a couple of fried eggs and a slab of country bacon—"

"Bring me the short stack," Jeff said. "Two eggs over easy, black coffee, and a couple of sausage patties. Do you have Rice's sausage?"

The woman was about fifty, old enough to be his mother. She looked at him as tolerantly as if she were.

"I'll tell you what, hon," she said. "I'm gonna bring you a plate of sausage that would make a hog proud to die. If you want to play like it's Rice's, nobody will hear a peep out of me." She called his order through the window.

Six minutes later she placed before him the biggest wheat cake the likes of which he never saw. It really did "lop over the sides," almost touching the Formica counter top. She brought a small glass pitcher of Aunt Jemima's maple syrup and the promised plate of sausage patties.

"You know," she said, pouring his cup full of black coffee. "I've fed about everybody in this town, and some of their dogs, but I don't remember seeing you in here before. You gonna stay a while, or you just passing through?"

"You could say that."

"I could say what?"

"I won't be here long."

"On your way to where?"

"St. Louis. I'm going to see about a job."

"What kind of job?"

In his thirty-two years Jeff added one-hundred-seventy-three pounds to the eight with which he entered the world. Many of those pounds found their way onto his six-foot frame by way of his addiction to hotcakes and sausage. Most of them he consumed in small diners like Dottie's because their hotcakes were better than the big chains'. But never had he encountered such a nosy waitress as this one.

"Radio," he said. "KMOX."

In the town of Marlow, fascination for radio and television personalities ranked only slightly below that of movie stars. Dottie was flattered that this one planted his backside on one of her stools, snarfing hotcakes and sausage at one o'clock in the afternoon.

"Radio, huh?" she beamed. "Isn't that Bruce Hayward on one of those radio stations in St. Louis? My, but I do love to hear that old boy talk. He's got the sexiest voice I ever heard on a man. Why, if I were twenty years younger—"

"Could I have some more butter, please?"

CHAPTER 3

Red Car Shock

At her desk outside Mason Bryer's door, Sally Hargis was filing her nails. It was Thursday afternoon. Until past midnight, they fed newsprint into the ancient cylindrical press that printed four pages at a time.

Those pages were given time to dry, then were flipped over and fed through again, and printed on the other side.

That morning, Sally and Bryer wrapped and mailed ninety-three copies of The Marlow Voice to out-of-town subscribers.

Bill Jessup, the typesetter, and Gig Goetze the pressman, were gone. Tomorrow they would be back to begin producing next week's edition. But now, it was Thursday afternoon, and for Sally it was a time for filing nails.

A neat, sharp-faced woman of forty-seven, black hair molded into a tight knot at the back of her head, she never married. She adored every ounce of Mason Bryer's two-hundred-ninety-four pounds of lard. To Sally, Mason was a gentle, considerate mountain of flesh whom only she understood. She fancied herself a buffer between Bryer and the rest of the free world.

At the sound of her master's voice, Sally leaped to her feet and bounced the nail file off the top of her desk. She pressed her palms along her thighs, straightened her black wool skirt, and eased open the door to Bryer's office.

"Yes, Mr. Bryer?" she said.

Mason locked his eyes on that red Corvette parked in front of Dottie's Diner. "Come look out this window," he said, waving her into the office. "Tell me what you see?"

"Out the window?"

"Yes, out the window. Just tell me the first thing that catches your eye."

Sally moved over to take a look. "There's the Gem Theater."

"No, no, farther down."

"I see the— Oh! There's a red car!"

"Hot damn!" Bryer hooted. "I hope Amos Marlow sees that red car. That old bastard will split a gut!"

The Monarch Speaks

From his office window on the second floor of

the Marlow Building, Amos Marlow kept a close watch on what took place on the city square. His eyes roved from the Bank of Marlow, which he owned; Abe Goldman's Jewelry; Cal Webster's Ladies Shoes and Ready-to-Wear; Herb Spencer's Haircut Shop; Lyle Foster's Bakery; and so on around the square. All the merchants paid monthly rent to Amos because he owned the buildings where their businesses were located.

And with pride, Amos enjoyed an unobstructed view of the twenty-four foot bronze statue of his stern-faced grandfather, Silas, glaring down at him from atop the City Hall tower.

If today Amos saw something on the street that he didn't see the day before, his goatee and pencil-thin mustache suffered an acute attack of the nervous twitches, and he wanted to know why it was there. Yesterday that red car, to which his beady black eyes were drawn, was not parked in front of Dottie's Diner.

To the phone Amos dashed, and into it he shouted, "What the hell is that red car doing out there on the street, Mr. Petty?"

Chink Petty carried the law in Marlow. He was the only peace officer the city ever had, and wouldn't have yet if Amos hadn't agreed to pay for it. The city budget provided no funds for law enforcement because, the city fathers rationalized, they never had it before, and the prospects for needing a gun-toter in their sleepy, God-fearing city were slim to none.

All of Chink's forty-two years he spent in Marlow, attended public school, took Zelda Lane to wed. Zelda presented him with four strapping sons, for whom he proudly claimed responsibility. Chink learned early where lay the power in the city of Marlow, but never dreamed he'd be a part of it.

As "the law in Marlow," as he was wont to say with nose sniffing pride, Chink "walked a fine line between the law and the outlaw." Ever mindful was he of Amos Marlow, the source of bread and butter with which Chink kept his wife and kids alive and kicking.

In his City Hall office, Chink's lanky frame leaned back in his swivel chair and stacked his Justin-booted feet on top of his desk. He lodged the phone between his left shoulder and his chin then lit up a Camel.

"What red car is that, sir?" Chink said into the phone.

"What red car is that?" Amos was in a dither. "Do you mean to sit there on your skinny ass and tell me you haven't seen that red car parked in front of Dottie's?"

"Well, sir, I've been pretty busy."

"Busy? I'll show you busy if you don't start keeping a closer watch on what goes on in this town. If the job is too much for you, we might have to do something about that."

Chink had heard it all before. In eight years on the job he'd adapted to Amos's childish outbursts and developed a philosophical immunity to the little man's explosive temperament. Amos was only asserting his authority, and the elderly gentleman with the twitching goatee was entitled. As long as he continued to pay Chink's salary, the deputy would put up with his verbal abuse.

Into the phone, Chink said, "I guess I must have missed that one."

"Missed that one! You must have missed that one?"

Amos was beside himself, and his mustache began performing its version of a windmill.

"What in hell do you think I pay you for?" he said.

"Well, Mr. Marlow, I—"

"Now, you listen closely to what I have to say to you. I want you to get over there to Dottie's Diner and find out who that red car belongs to and report back to me. Do you think you can handle that, Mr. Petty?"

Amos called him Mr. Petty any time he thought Chink needed to be reminded who was in charge.

"I'll get on it right away, sir."

"You just keep in mind how you got to be the law in this town, and maybe that'll help you get it done."

Chink plunked down the phone and headed for the door.

He passed Liz Barnes's desk, and said, "Shut up."

Liz grinned and kept typing.

CHAPTER 4

Who is Susie McCord?

Jeff handed the woman a twenty-dollar bill.

"I bet you're Dottie," he said.

"In the flesh, hon."

She placed the twenty in the cash drawer and came out with a handful of change.

"I've been here seventeen years, ever since that idiot I was married to ran off with that red-headed manicurist and left me with two little girls to raise on my own." With a mischievous grin, she said, "Are you married, hon?"

Jeff took his change and shook his head no.

"I was just joshing about being married," Dottie grinned. "Both my kids are up and gone. Sometimes they bring their babies home to Grandma's. I don't see much of them anymore. They used to help me out here a lot, but I've been doing it all since

Susie—"

Their eyes met, hers unblinking, afraid she had said too much.

Jeff held her gaze. Strange that she would mention Susie's name—the one he saw on the billboard.

"Any chance that would have something to do with Susie McCord?" he said.

"What's your name, hon?"

"Timberlake. Jeff. I saw the sign,"

"Well, Timberlake Jeff, I'm mighty proud you stopped by my place today. I hope you'll come again next time you feel the need to stuff your innards with the world's greatest wheat cakes and sausage."

He watched her face. Behind that nervous grin she was hiding something. She was afraid. Of what?

"You know about Susie, don't you?" he said.

Dottie tossed a quick glance at the half dozen customers seated around tables. They were stuffing themselves, paying no attention to what was going on at the counter. Even so, her answer was a whisper.

"Everybody knows about Susie," she said, "but what they know and what they tell are not always the same."

Jeff nodded, trying to see past the uncertainty in her eyes. He picked up a copy of The Marlow Voice off the counter by the cash register and handed Dottie a dime for it.

"You won't find the answer in there," she said. "You seem like a nice man, and I'd hate to see anything bad happen to you, so I'll give you a little friendly advice. You need to be mighty careful who you talk to about this. To some in this town, the plague is more welcome than a stranger. Especially a stranger who asks questions about Susie McCord."

The Law Arrives in Khaki Pants

Petty could have walked from his office to Dottie's Diner across the square in less time than it took him to climb into the cruiser and drive there. But to him, the white Ford Fairlane was more impressive than his khaki pants and shirt, even with the badge attached. Besides that, the flashing lights and gold shields stenciled on the sides of the cruiser bolstered his confidence and made him feel like he was in charge.

Chink made an illegal U-turn at the light on Main Street and parked in front of Dottie's. The red Corvette was not there.

Chink unwound his six-foot frame from the cruiser and ambled in through Dottie's door. He greeted her with a casual wave, and planted his rear end on the same stool Jeff Timberlake vacated minutes before. Petty was proud to be "a servant of the people of Marlow," and often called that to Dottie's attention when he dropped by for free coffee and donuts, to which he considered himself entitled as a servant of the people. He and Dottie had known each other forever. Zelda made the blueberry pies Dottie served at the diner. Marlow was so uncriminal nobody felt the need for protection by the law until eight years ago. That was when Honus Goddard crushed his wife Emmy between the front porch and his Chevy pickup because she burned the biscuits.

Honus was convicted of "premeditated mayhem," translated by the judge as first degree murder, and was sentenced to life in prison.

Even so, some Marlow folks were afraid Honus might come back to wreak havoc on the town. They decided it would be a good idea to have somebody out there looking out for them. Burnt biscuits being a blight on the face of the earth, however, some sympathized with what Honus did to Emmy. You never knew when some off-his-rocker idiot might go berserk and mow down somebody else's wife.

Sheriff Clay Mitchell had all he could take care of out in the county, and "we need one of our own," the locals cried.

Chink got the nod.

Nobody questioned whether Chink was qualified to handle the job of keeping the peace in Marlow. After all, he served two years as deputy to Mitchell. And Chink saw every one of John Wayne's movies, and even developed to perfection the Duke's sideways walk. Not to mention that time in Springfield when he bid forty dollars for the shirt Wayne wore in "Stagecoach".

Chink lost his bid for the shirt to somebody who bid $42.00. Being there, and bidding on it gave him stature. He felt cowboyish in his Justin boots and white flat-top Stetson hat. His revolver rode low on his right thigh, inspiring townsfolk to dub him "the marshal."

Chink liked that.

Marlowites paraded in the streets to the beat of the high school band, expressing their gratitude for being blessed with one of their own on the job twenty four/seven, protecting them from pickup-wielding maniacs like Honus Goddard.

Jubilation took a serious turn for the worse when it was discovered the city of Marlow had no money to pay for a lawman. City fathers, prompted by the local outcry, were forced to come up with the money or go without a peace keeper, threatening the locals with the risk of getting crushed between something and a pickup truck.

As a last resort, the mayor formed a circle with friends around his desk, dropped to their knees, clutched each other's hands, intoned Kumbaya, and appealed to a Higher Power.

To their surprise and gratitude, their entreaties engendered an immediate response beyond their wildest dreams. Accompanied by boundless joy, that very afternoon, in the doorway of Mayor Foxworthy's office appeared an angel bearing gifts in the form of a commitment to foot the bill for the services of the newly appointed deputy, Chink Petty. The angel was Waldo, Amos Marlow's black chauffeur, dispatched to rescue the fathers from the perils of the outer darkness.

In a special ceremony on the town square, the grateful city showered Amos with praise and thanksgiving, lauding the fine civic gesture of the town's leading citizen. The people of Marlow, joined by Sheriff Clay Mitchell and County Attorney Blake Baldwin, listened in reverent silence as the mayor commended Amos for his public spirited generosity.

The mayor awarded Amos a gold-plated unicorn pipe lighter which ever after adorned the mahogany desk in Amos's office. Amos assumed the responsibility for Chink's salary which, some said, so endeared him to the marshal.

To this day it is not clear whether Chink's move toward Dottie's Diner to investigate the appearance of a strange red car on the public square was prompted by the marshal's devotion to his civic duty, or by his allegiance to the man who provided food and shelter for his wife and kids. Chink tried not to distinguish one from the other.

After the phone call from Amos, Chink struck a beeline for Dottie's.

Through her front window, Dottie saw him coming. By the time Chink plopped down on that stool, she poured his coffee and doctored it with cream and two spoonsful of sugar. She slid the cup and saucer along the counter, planning the shot so it stopped directly in front of the marshal.

"Howdy, Marshal," Dottie said. "What the hell are you doing up this time of day? I thought you'd be home taking your beauty nap by now."

"Couldn't sleep," Petty drawled.

Chink ripped a paper napkin from the chrome dispenser and wiped coffee drippings off his chin. Habit forced him to glance around at the other diners. He saw no one he hadn't seen before.

"Listen, Dottie," Chink said. "Did you see that red car parked out there a while ago?"

"You think I wouldn't notice a red Corvette parked in front of my place?"

"A Corvette?" He whistled through his teeth. "That's what it was?"

"That's what it was."

"Bunch of bucks tied up in that one. Do you know who it belonged to?"

"Who wants to know?"

"I do."

From the tops of her green eyes, she laid on him a dubious look. "You and who else?"

"Now, come on, Dottie, you've been around long enough to know how things work in this town."

"I know how things work, and I know who pays you to work 'em. How much longer is it going to take you to learn when he gets through with you, he'll throw you on the same garbage heap he's paying you to hide?"

"You sound like Zelda."

"That wife of yours is not dumb enough to believe he keeps you around for your pretty face." She grinned. "Even if she was dumb enough to marry you."

"Yeah, well, we all have our crosses to bear, don't we? Zelda knows where the bread and butter come from. "Dottie, about that red Corvette."

Dottie wasn't about to utter the name of Jeff Timberlake. She pegged him as a nice young man who deserved better than what might happen to him if Amos found out who he was and why he was in town. Neither was she going to tell the local gendarme, pawn of Amos Marlow, anything that might get Jeff in trouble. She liked Chink, but she didn't come close to telling him who the red Corvette belonged to. She'd auction off one of her grandkids before she'd feed Amos's paranoia about red cars.

She looked the marshal squarely in the eye, and said, "You tell that old devil if I hear anything I think he needs to know, I'll send a runner. And tell him to keep that brat of a grandson of his out of my place, or next time he's in here I'm calling the cop and having him hauled away."

Chink's ears perked up. "Has Randy been acting up again?"

"You might call it acting up. I call it tearing up. Randy-pandy gets a few beers in his belly, and why he winds up here I don't know. He brings a buddy or two with him and acts like he's got to prove something. He rips the covers off my stools and smashes my water glasses against the wall. That stool you're sitting on I just had recovered for the third time."

"Have you talked to his mama about that?" Chink said. "Jackie has always been good about taking care of stuff like that."

"That heifer! I have trouble communicating with the village punch board. We don't speak the same language."

"Now, Dottie—"

"Don't now Dottie me, Chink. I'd give half my interest in hell for the chance Jackie Marlow had. I'll give her daddy that much. She had the world on a silver platter after her mama died in that car wreck. All Jackie had to do was straighten up and fly right, but she never amounted to a hoot in a hailstorm."

"Mr. Marlow was looking for something too,

you know," Chink said. "He's not the same person since his wife died."

"He hasn't been the same since the day he was born. Demented old coot!"

"You might want to be careful who you say that to."

"I know, Chink, and I'm sorry he lost his wife, but he doesn't have to take it out on the whole town. We didn't kill her, for crying out loud! And that daughter of his—you know as well as I do, she took success and turned it into an overnight disaster. And that bastard kid of hers grew up to be just like her—no damn good!"

"Well, Randy went back to MU for the fall semester."

"That's too damn bad," Dottie spat. "He'll be missed."

"You can't blame Randy too much. He's a little wild, like most kids his age."

"He's not a kid any more. When I was twenty-one, I was busting my backside to support a no-good husband and two little girls."

"Yeah, well, Randy pretty much walked the line until—" He caught her eye then looked away.

"Until what, Chink?" She leaned across the counter and pinned him with a hard gaze. "Until Susie?"

"Now, Dottie, there's no use digging all that up again."

"Well, it's high time somebody dug it up again. This town has clammed up too damn long to protect that kid."

"We don't know everything."

"No, and the way things are going we'll never find out. But we know Randy took Susie home from that party. He admitted that much. Just because he was too drunk to remember anything else doesn't make him innocent."

"It's all over, Dottie. Dead and buried."

"Susie McCord is dead and buried. And I have an idea somebody else ought to be."

"You can say that, but everybody in this town owes Amos Marlow. Don't forget that. If it wasn't for him, there wouldn't be any town."

"Yeah, and if it wasn't for mosquitoes there wouldn't be any typhoid either."

"Anybody who doesn't like it can go someplace else."

"I can't go someplace else," she said. "Everything I own is what you're sitting on!"

Chink removed his backside from Dottie's stool.

"I've got to go," he said. "Mr. Marlow—" He cast her a sheepish glance. "I'll see you later, Dottie."

"Yeah. Tell Zelda to hang in there. Some day you may grow up to be the man she thought she married."

CHAPTER 5

The Search for Zachary Wheeler

Jeff pulled to the curb and asked a wiry little old man hobbling along the sidewalk with a walking stick where he'd find Oak Street.

"Oak Street, you say?"

"Yes, sir."

"Oak Street runs north and south." He waved his walking stick to his right. "Three blocks over that way. But there's not anything over there you'll want to see."

Jeff waved thanks and drove away.

He found Oak Street and braked to a stop in front of 311. The old man was right. Three-eleven was a rundown two-story frame house he guessed was once an imposing mansion. The wrought iron fence encircling the bare dirt yard appeared to be the only thing that survived the ravages of time. Holes bigger than fists punctured the front screen door, and the windows were covered with card-board. Through the gate and up the crumbling concrete walk he strode to the front porch, questioning whether this could be the home of Zachary Wheeler.

He checked the address on his mother's envelope, and knocked on the door.

The door creaked open a crack. In it stood a young woman with stringy brown hair. On her right hip was lodged a small child in a smelly diaper.

"Yes?" the woman said.

Most people who knocked on her door wanted something—like rent money. And sometimes the sheriff sent a deputy to investigate a report of mistreatment by an alcoholic husband. Jeff's eyes couldn't miss the bruises on the young woman's face that told him she hadn't escaped what he suspected was her husband's abuse.

"What is it?" she said.

"I'm sorry to bother you. My name is Jeff Timberlake. I'm trying to locate a man named Zachary Wheeler. I was given this address."

"Who? Wheeler?" She shook her head. "Ain't nobody here by that name."

"You don't know a man named Zachary Wheeler?"

She turned her head to the inside of the house, as if seeking help from someone Jeff couldn't see.

"We've been here seven years," she said. "I never heard of anybody named Wheeler."

Jeff nodded. "Thanks. Could I ask you one more thing?"

"I guess so."

"Did you know Susie McCord?" The woman appeared startled by the question. From inside the house, Jeff heard a man's gruff voice.

"What's he talking about?"

"He's asking about Susie," the woman said.

Seconds later the man, unshaved and red-eyed, shoved the woman aside and filled the doorway with his hulk, hairy and naked from the waist up.

"We don't know nothing about that," he said to Jeff.

"You can't tell me anything about Susie McCord?"

The man took the cigarette from the corner of his mouth and pointed it at Jeff. "We don't know nothing about no Susie McCord, and I wouldn't tell you if I did," he said, pushing the door open. "Now you get the hell off my front porch."

Jeff gave him a startled stare, decided he would do better not to pursue the matter, and got the hell off his front porch.

Jeff's curiosity went for a wild spin. The red-eyed man with the hairy chest didn't look like he'd be easily intimidated. Even so, Jeff was convinced that he too was afraid of something.

Jeff settled under the wheel of the Corvette, and studied his mother's sealed envelope on the seat beside him. He turned it over and back again. How urgent was it? Would Wheeler care if he never got it?

The answers didn't come, but it didn't matter. Recalling the pleading in his mother's eyes, Jeff knew it was important to her that Wheeler get the letter.

He would put St. Louis on the back burner for a couple of days and try to find someone who knew of Zachary Wheeler. The mystery of Susie McCord wouldn't go away. Who was she? How did she die? Why did he care?

Rarely did he bother to analyze why he did whatever he did. Unlike the man who scaled the mountain "because it was there," Jeff's rationale was "why not?" The need to find out what happened to Susie McCord kept gnawing at his insides. He was struck by the reality that uncovering the mystery was becoming more than just his professional concern for the death of a young girl nobody wanted to talk about.

Welcome to the E-Z Rest

Linus Gibbs looked out his front window and saw a red Corvette pulling into a parking spot in front of his E-Z-Rest Motel. A sandy haired young man got out of the car. He looked around, as though questioning whether this place was where he wanted to be. Linus watched him push open the front door.

Jeff Timberlake was a sturdily built, good looking six-footer, blessed with a smooth, sun-tanned complexion. Men liked him, and women were drawn to him, an onus he bore with limited modesty throughout his career as a broadcaster. He left no grape to wither on the vine.

To Linus Jeff looked like a man who was used to more class than the E-Z Rest offered.

A nice lady raking leaves in her front yard directed Jeff to the motel on the edge of town.

"It's the only one we have," she told him.

Behind the counter stood the baggy-eyed proprietor with the stub end of a dead cigar sticking out the corner of his mouth. Jeff was not impressed by the faded green T-shirt that stopped a couple of inches short of Linus's turquoise belt buckle, exposing a strip of white flab.

Behind Linus slumped a faded gray sofa strewn with newspapers and outdated copies of Playboy. Beside the sofa, a wooden table was littered with half a dozen coffee-stained cups and a brass ashtray full of smelly cigar butts.

"Do you have a room?" Jeff said, half wishing he were someplace else.

He peered about in search of an escape hatch. In a trap like the E-Z Rest, he might need it to make a quick getaway.

"How long you gonna be here?" Linus wanted to know.

Jeff wondered if that was a qualification for whether he had a room. "I don't know," Jeff said. "Maybe a couple of days. I'm supposed to see a man named Zachary Wheeler."

Linus spun the guest book around for him to sign.

"There used to be a man around here named Wheeler," the innkeeper said. "He came from someplace else and never spent much time here in town. He traveled for Abe Goldman. Sold jewelry on the road. I guess business got bad, and I never seen Wheeler no more. I don't know what happened to him after that. Seems like somebody said he died, but that was a long time ago. Abe had a store down on the square. Abe's gone, but the store's still there. Leland Haymes owns it now. Of course, Leland pays rent to Amos Marlow. About everybody in town does."

"You don't know what happened to Zachary Wheeler?"

Linus shook his head. "Not any more. It's been a long time." Jeff signed the book.

"That'll be eight dollars a night," Linus said. "The first night in advance."

Jeff laid out a ten-dollar bill. Linus dragged a King Edward cigar box from under the counter, took out two crumpled one-dollar bills and handed them to Jeff. Jeff stuffed them in a pocket. "I guess you don't know anything about Susie McCord either?" Jeff asked.

"Who?"

Jeff couldn't believe Linus's hearing was that bad. "I saw the Susie sign out on the highway. It's pretty unusual. I wondered why it was there. Do you know anything about that?"

Linus took some time to think that over. "You must be new around here," he said.

Jeff flicked the corner of his mouth into a token smile. If he hadn't been new around there he wouldn't have to ask about Susie. And he wouldn't be put-ting out eight dollars a night for a bed at the sleazy E-Z.

"Yes," Jeff said. "I just got in town."

"All I know is what folks around here say," Linus said.

"And what do folks around here say?"

Linus glanced down at the name Jeff wrote in the book.

"You're from Dez Moines?" he said.

"That's right."

"I had a cousin who lived in Dez Moines once. He had a nice business going. He done real good as long as he kept his mouth shut. Then he got to doing so good he had to talk about it. He bragged to anybody who'd listen about what a good deal he had, and how much money he was making.

"One day they found him dead in a parking lot. Throat cut. Buried in a pile of greenbacks."

Jeff saw in Linus's eyes the same fear that Dottie tried to hide behind her smile. "Does that mean you don't know anything about Susie McCord?"

"What that means is, this motel is the only thing in the world with my name on it," Linus said. "The bank owns most of it, but my wife and I make a pretty good living off it, and we can't afford to lose it."

He shifted his eyes from side to side as if afraid of being overheard, though there was no one else around. "I don't know why that sign keeps standing out there on the highway," Linus said. "But if I was in your shoes, I wouldn't go looking for somebody who does."

Jeff gave his head a dubious shake.

The city of Marlow was blanketed in a cloud of fear. He heard it in their voices, and saw it in their eyes. From somewhere inside him, a voice kept shouting, "Why?"

The one luxury in his room at the E-Z Rest was a

telephone. He picked it up and dialed. On the other end, a nice lady with a pleasant voice, said, "National News Service. How may I direct your call?"

"Charlene Gore, please."

"Certainly, sir. One moment, please."

Charlene Gore was the Des Moines bureau chief of National News Service. She and Jeff exchanged tips and details of breaking news stories when he was at WHO Radio. Charlene was a professional friend with an uncanny instinct for sniffing out a story.

"This is Charlene," said a voice on the phone.

"Jeff Timberlake."

"Jeff! Where are you?"

"You'd never guess. See if you can find Marlow, Missouri, on your map."

"Just a minute. You said Marlow? Yeah, here it is, about half way between Deer Crossing and Resume Speed. What the hell are you doing in Marlow, Missouri?"

"It's a long story. I'll tell you about it sometime. You know *who* and I split."

"Yeah, I heard about that. So, what do you want—a job? I've been trying to get you obligated to me for years."

"There's something screwy going on in this town."

"How screwy?"

"Out on the highway there's a sign advertising the death of a girl named Susie McCord. I thought there might be a story behind it."

"There's a story behind everything, Jeff. Are you

thinking foul play, human interest, what?"

"I don't know yet. There's not much to go on, except that nobody wants to talk about it. My bones tell me there's something smelly going on here."

"Well, I can't print your bones, Jeff, but if you think we can use it, go for it. Do you want me to send you some money?"

"We can talk about that later. Right now I need a reason to go snooping around."

"You've got it. Tell them you're snooping for NNS."

"Thanks. I'll call you."

"Pick you later."

Jeff hung up, and slumped into his chair.

Who was Susie McCord?

CHAPTER 6

Hear the Word of the Lord

Ethan Timberlake was a fire and brimstone preacher who revered the Holy Bible as the indisputable Word of God. "If you tamper with part of it," he proclaimed with the fervor of John the Baptist waist deep in the Jordan River, "you dilute all of it!"

The precepts of Christianity "are all a body needs to live a fruitful, God-fearing life. If you have no guilt, you have no fear!"

Jeff's long suffering mother Leota never questioned the authority of her husband's ramblings. Whether it was because she subscribed to the truth of Ethan's fiery oratory, or because she feared arousing his wrath by challenging his preachments, Jeff didn't know. Even so, he and his father were poles apart on many subjects.

Jeff carried with him yet the bitter memories of cringing as a young boy at the sight of bodies "in the grasp of the Holy Spirit," groveling in the dust of a camp meeting tent, frothing at the mouth like rabid dogs. Caught up in the threat of hellfire and damnation—"if you don't get right with God right now!"—converts, trembling arms reaching for the heavens, screaming and moaning in hypnotic trances, babbling sounds even they didn't understand.

Jeff left home after high school. He hated leaving his mother, whom he dearly loved, but he felt no remorse for separating himself from his scripture-spouting father.

Three days ago Jeff patted the limp arm of his dying mother as she folded into his palm the small white envelope addressed to Zachary Wheeler. Jeff buried her beside her husband. He came away with a head full of questions about what took place between Leota and Wheeler. He could only guess the answers.

Now, both parents gone, Jeff had no ties to any place he could call "home." At no time did he consider taking up residence at the E-Z Rest Motel in Marlow, Missouri.

It wasn't much of a room. Against one beige painted wall stood an iron bedstead with peeling green paint. A black telephone sat on a small wooden table beside the bed, and an ancient overstuffed chair stood near the door.

There was no tub in the bathroom, and water from the shower drained into a hole in the concrete floor. Unlike the overnight palaces by which such drabness would one day be replaced, motel patrons in 1958 paid for no luxury, and received none.

On his way out, Jeff threw open the door. He was startled to see standing in it a tall thin man with a fist poised as if about to knock. A brass badge was pinned above the man's khaki shirt pocket, and low on his right thigh rode a pistol in a leather holster.

"Chink Petty," the man said. "Police."

Jeff couldn't believe he'd been in Marlow long enough to get cross-ways with the law.

"Have I done something wrong, Mr. Petty?" he said.

"Don't know yet. We need to talk about that."

"Do you want to come in?"

Jeff stood aside and waved Petty into the room.

"We can start with your name," Petty said.

"Jeff Timberlake. Would you like to sit down? It's not much of a room, but—" He waited for some reaction that told him Petty's hearing was not faulty, but got none.

Petty stood in the doorway, surveying the room with a curious eye as if he never saw anything like it before—as if he expected to find evidence that Jeff committed some horrible crime.

"So, what are we going to talk about, Mr. Petty?"

"Do you own that red car parked outside?"

"The Corvette? Sure."

"That's what we're going to talk about."

"Why? Is there a law against red cars in this town?"

Chink favored him with a wry smile. "You got a reason for staying overnight?"

"I've got a reason."

The marshal waited. "Well, what is it?"

"I get the feeling I'm not welcome in this town," Jeff said, "and I wonder why."

"Folks around here look at strangers kind of sideways 'til they find out what they're up to."

"Do you think I'm up to something?"

Petty stared at him, and gave him a tolerant nod. "Marlow is a small town, Mr. Timberlake. Not much changes here. It's been that way a long time. Not many strangers decide to stay."

"So?"

"So, whatever you're here for, get it done."

"What I'm here for is a private matter. What is it about red cars?"

"Some say red is a sign of bad luck."

"What do you say, Mr. Petty?"

"A law enforcement officer can't take sides."

"Uh-huh. Do any of these people you refer to have names?"

Chink viewed him with a jaundiced eye. "Why do you want to know?"

"I'd like to talk to them."

"About what?"

"Susie McCord."

Petty hardly flinched. "Susie's dead," he said.

"I know. What I don't know is how she died, and why her death would be advertised on a billboard out there on the highway."

Petty lifted his hand in a gesture of finality. "Whatever you're here for," he said, "don't take too long."

Petty opened the door and walked out. Without a backward glance, the marshal climbed into his black-and-white cruiser, and sped away with its lights flashing.

Jeff closed the door and gave his head a bewildered shake. If Petty was chairman of the Marlow city welcoming committee, it was no surprise that "not many people decide to stay."

On the bed he spied the copy of The Marlow Voice he paid a dime for at Dottie's. He grabbed it up and headed out the door to pay his respects to Mason Bryer, the one person in town who shouldn't be bashful about talking to him.

What Happened at WHO?

In the unhurried days of the 1950's a man could work at a radio station for a few months and salt away enough money to move on to a more attractive job in a bigger city where the pay was better. Some aspiring stars stayed at one radio station for a few weeks only, always in pursuit of the "Big Break." Their ambition gave rise to a class of broadcasters dubbed "radio bums." With an eye on the road ahead, hopefully every move was a rung up the ladder to fame and fortune.

Jeff spent four years under the critical gaze of Marvin Huddleston. He didn't include himself among the short timers. Still, like every radio personality with a breath of ambition, Jeff harbored the dream of one day being discovered by some network talent scout or TV star taken by his sparkling on-air personality, or the pear-shaped tones of his dulcet voice.

Around the next bend in the road, or under the

transmitter tower reaching for the sky on the hill ahead, a star-studded future may be awaiting his arrival. Jeff's talents served him well until, on a recent Friday afternoon, he said "whore" on the radio. For that breach of broadcasting etiquette he received from Marvin Huddleston a prompt and irrevocable invitation to depart the premises.

Jeff knew it was against the law of propriety to utter that word on the air, especially in the heart of the Midwest Bible Belt. Such words offended the delicate scripture-oriented ears attuned to one of mid-America's most powerful radio stations. Other prohibitions included "condom" and "penis." "Hell" and "damn" were verboten, and "rape" and "sex" were uttered only in smoke-filled, vermin-infested back rooms. Even "harass" was too suggestive of worldly pleasures if the second syllable was emphasized.

Jeff knew that. It was a rule. It wasn't written down any place, and nobody ever talked about it, but you just didn't say "whore" on the radio.

He did, because that's what the woman in the news story he was reporting was. Some inner voice screamed at him, "She is not a call girl, she is not a lady of the evening, nor any of those euphemisms at which Bible-oriented listeners would not apoplectic.

"She's a whore!"

So, he said it. Out loud. On the radio—for all of heartland America to hear and disbelieve. Stewing outside the studio door, waiting for Jeff to finish the story and break for a commercial, Huddleston's head almost came unglued. As soon as the On-Air light went out, fat Marvin rolled in.

"The switchboard is lit up like a Christmas tree," he screamed at Jeff. "What the hell did you say?"

Jeff never cared for Marvin anyway.

Now, here he was, a stranger in an unfriendly town, obsessed by what happened to a young girl about whom he knew nothing, except that she was dead.

With a wry smile, he suffered no regrets for separating himself from the lard-assed Huddleston.

Jeff circled the square until he spotted The Voice office four doors down from the Marlow Building. He parked the Corvette in front then went inside. A prim, half-old woman greeted him from her desk beside a door with Mason Bryer's name on it.

"How can I help you?" the woman said.

"I'd like to see Mr. Bryer."

"Mr. Bryer is not in," she said. "I'm Mr. Bryer's assistant. Perhaps I can help you, Mister—"

"Timberlake. Jeff Timberlake, National News Service."

"I'm Miss Hargis," she said, extending her little white hand.

Timberlake pressed her limp fingers in a mechanical handshake.

"I saw the sign out on the highway about Susie McCord," he said. "I couldn't help wondering why it's there. I thought Mr. Bryer might fill me in on the details."

"As I said, Mr. Bryer is—" She stood up as if through talking.

"Miss Hargis, I'm on assignment to find out what caused Susie's death," Jeff said. "I'd really appreciate it if you could show me pictures, school reports, death certificate, obituary, anything at all about the death of Susie McCord."

Sally couldn't remember the last time anyone inquired about Susie. "That was a long time ago," she said.

"How long?"

"Four years. It was 1954."

"You remember it that well?"

Miss Hargis gave him a look that said she'd rather not talk about it. Anyway, she thought, why would a reputable company like National News Service care what happened in a one-horse town like Marlow, Missouri? Especially that long ago.

She was reminded of the frustration Susie's death caused her boss. She wasn't eager to talk about it to some stranger who wandered in off the street, claimed be from a news service that would spread it all over the country.

"I don't think I can do anything for you," she said. "Perhaps when Mr. Bryer returns—"

"Didn't you publish an account of Susie's death? An obituary, funeral arrangements, anything?"

"Ah—" she hedged. "No. There's nothing in the archives about the death of Susie McCord."

"Well, now isn't that a bit unusual? A young girl dies in a small town, and it doesn't even make the obit column?"

"I'm sorry, Mr. Timberlake. I really think you'd better talk with Mr. Bryer about that."

"Miss Hargis, you know about these things." It couldn't hurt to sprinkle a little sugar along the path of one whose help he needed. "You know the town, you know the people," he went on. "Your newspaper is the main source of information, and I don't have much time. Actually, I've been threatened with arrest if I stay around too long."

"Threatened? By whom?"

"Some guy with a badge named Chink Petty. He has something against red cars."

"Oh. You drive a red car?"

"A Corvette."

The one Mr. Bryer called her to look for out the window. She turned her head away, muttering something that sounded like "Amos Marlow."

"I'm sorry," Jeff said. Linus mentioned that name too. "I'm not sure I heard what you said."

"Am— The marshal wasn't acting on his own."

"Who is Amos Marlow?"

"I'm afraid I can't help you, Mr. Timberlake."

"Is there someone I can talk to about Susie? A friend, relative, an acquaintance?"

Sally gave that a moment of silent consideration. This man was sincere. He showed a genuine interest in the fate of Susie McCord. Her boss struggled with the Susie thing for four years without success because of people's fear of retribution from Amos Marlow. She didn't know if Jeff Timberlake was who he said he was, but if he should uncover something that would help ease Mr. Bryer's frustration, she'd take the chance his claim was legitimate.

"Amy Kraft," Sally said abruptly. "At the high school. That's all I can tell you."

She ushered him to the door, and closed it behind him. For a long moment she leaned against the door and pressed her palms along her thighs as if to cleanse them of some frightful disease.

Jeff pulled the Corvette into a Texaco station and was greeted by a young black man wearing a broad grin and a St. Louis Cardinals baseball cap.

"Hep ye, sir?" the young man said.

"Fill 'er up," Jeff said, "and tell me how to get to the school."

When he came for the money, Jeff handed the man a couple of bills.

The attendant removed his cap and scratched his head with the same hand. "You the one asking about Susie?"

"That's right. How did you know that?"

"The red car."

Jeff nodded as if he understood, but really didn't.

What was it about red cars in this town? Did they post lookouts for strange cars, sounding the alarm to alert the natives any time a red one was spotted? He visualized people all over town peeking out from behind drawn shades, eye-balling his every move.

"Have you found out anything?" the attendant said.

"Not much."

"Ain't no surprise. Nobody knows anything."

"Is that so?"

"Well, see, you gotta be in on what's happening here."

"Okay. What is happening here?" Jeff said.

"In this town they's the big people, and the little people. The big people live on this side of the river, and the little people live on the other side. The only time they mix is when the big people boys cross the bridge to pick on the little people boys to make sure we 'member where we belong.

"And sometimes they hit on the little people girls 'cause they think they easier than the big people girls. Know what I mean?"

Jeff nodded. "I'm working on it'"

"If they's ever any trouble, the little people get blamed for it, 'cause the law is paid by the big people that own all the stuff."

"And that's why nobody knows anything about Susie?"

"Right on!"

"Because the big people don't want you to tell."

The young man flashed a wide grin. "You got it!"

"You don't think I'm one of the big people?"

"Nah! You wouldn't be asking about Susie."

"Was Susie black?"

"Nah, she white like you. But she never acted like she was better'n us, see. Most of the white kids didn't want nothin' to do with us."

"You thought Susie was okay, though?"

"Oh, yeah, man. Susie was cool. Some of the whites didn't like her mixing with us, but she didn't care. Know what I mean?"

"I think so."

"Some of them jealous, you know, her being Homecoming Queen and all. And from the wrong side of the river too."

The young man glanced around, nervous about spending too much time talking to a stranger in a red car. He lifted his cap and scratched his head again.

"Well, see," he said, "they's people—if they saw me talking to you—"

"Okay, I'm out of here."

"You say you want to go to the school?"

"Yes. Do you know Amy Kraft?"

"Oh yeah, man! Miz Amy, she's a fine lady. She's the PE teacher."

He told Jeff how to get to the school on Walnut Street, and handed him his change.

Jeff said, "What's your name?"

"Hack Peebles."

Hack's smile disappeared. He watched the Corvette pull away, lifted his cap, and scratched his head.

"Don't get too close, man," Hack said out loud.

CHAPTER 7

Jeff Goes to School

Amy Kraft was twenty-nine years old. She had taught school for eight years, the last five at Marlow High.

Jeff found her in the gym, dismissing a class of girls in shorts and sweat tops.

Slender and athletic, Amy moved with the grace of a doe in her white gym shoes and Kelly green sweats. Her blond ponytail was tied with a green ribbon that matched her eyes. The pony tail bounced off her neck as she strode briskly to where Jeff was waiting near the entrance.

"I'm Amy Kraft," she said.

Jeff grasped the hand she held out to him. "Jeff Timberlake." He followed her to the cafeteria.

She slid into a booth and waved him to the seat opposite then asked a girl student, "Bring us a couple of Cokes." The girl brought them, then left.

Amy sipped at hers. "Somebody said you wanted to see me." Her mouth turned up at the corners in an easy smile. "What did you say your name was?"

"Jeff Timberlake."

"And what was it you wanted to talk to me about?"

"Miss Hargis at the newspaper office suggested I come see you."

"Sally put you onto me, did she?"

"She thought you might be able to tell me something about what happened to Susie McCord."

Amy's response was a sharp look. Jeff couldn't tell if it was a look of shock, resentment, or fear. He wondered if here was another one who wasn't going to tell him anything. What was it with these people? Dottie was afraid of saying too much, Linus didn't want to lose his motel, Hack feared reprisal from the "big people," and some irate redneck ordered him off his front porch. Even the local cop stoned up when he mentioned Susie's name. And now, sitting across from him, this gorgeous creature was shooting darts at him, green eyes daring him to pursue the subject of Susie McCord. "There seems to be some deep, dark secret about Susie's death," he said. "Can you tell me what it is?"

"You don't want to know."

There it was. The brick wall he couldn't see through. "That's not for you to decide," Jeff said.

"Leave it alone, Mr. Timberlake. Whatever happened to Susie is none of your business."

"A young girl dies; the paper has no account of it, and everybody, including the local gendarme, quakes at the sound of her name. Yet, out there on that highway a billboard tells the world that Susie McCord died here. Can you explain that?"

Amy didn't feel the need to explain anything to anybody, especially some man she never saw before, about a subject that people in Marlow didn't talk about. "It doesn't concern you," she said.

"Okay, let's say it doesn't concern me. Does it concern you, Miss Kraft, that a popular young girl dies in this town the size of a postage stamp and nobody cares about it?"

She rolled the Coke bottle between her palms, and looked at him like she would like to tell him everything she knew about Susie, but dared not.

"I'll tell you what, Mr. Timberlake—"

"Jeff."

"—Sally Hargis sent you out here so I could tell you to go to hell because she didn't have the guts to tell you herself."

"Why would she do that?"

Amy scanned his tanned face, the deep brown eyes, the dimple on the left side of his chin. *Why would a smart, good looking guy like him from God knows where care what happened to Susie McCord?*

"There are some things that people in this town don't talk about," Amy said, "especially with strangers. One of them is Susie McCord."

"Why is that?"

"I can tell you this much: Susie was one of the finest young girls I ever knew. She was a good athlete, made straight A's in school, and was never late to class. It's unbelievable that what happened to her is still a big mystery."

"What did happen to her?"

"Officially? Accidental drowning."

"You don't agree with that?"

"Let me tell you something, Mr. Timberlake." Her Irish eyes were not smiling. "I don't know what your problem is with this Susie thing, but I've got a good job here, and I can't afford to lose it because I talked to some guy about a girl who has been dead for four years. If you think I'm taking a chance on that, you're way past due for a head check."

From somewhere in the shadowy confines of Jeff's consciousness rose the Voice of Reason. It reminded him that when all else fails, you rise, fold your tent, and silently steal way.

The lady had said her piece. But he would see more of Amy Kraft.

The Deputy's Report

Chink Petty stood with his hat in his hand, looking down into the gray face of Amos Marlow.

From behind his huge mahogany desk adorned with the unicorn pipe lighter, Amos appraised the anxious expression on the marshal's face. Amos didn't like what he saw.

He grasped the unicorn, pressed the trigger, and held the flame to the bowl of his curve-stemmed pipe. The blue-green flame shot from the horse's mouth, igniting the rough cut burley. Amos puffed at his pipe, blew out a cloud of gray smoke, and eyed the lawman with a glare. He didn't invite the deputy to sit.

"So, what can you tell me?" Amos said, exhaling a fog of smoke.

"The man who owns that red Corvette is Jeff Timberlake. He's from Des Moines, just passing through town."

"You're sure he's just passing through?"

"Yes, sir," Chink said. "Some personal business he has to take care of, then he'll be gone."

Amos grunted, questioning Chink's ability to get at the truth. "Are you damn sure that he'll be gone?"

"I told him not to take too long."

"I guess if he moves on right away it can't amount to much."

Chink cleared his throat.

"Is there something more, Mr. Petty?"

"Well, sir, he did say something about Susie McCord."

Amos shot straight up out of his leather-bound chair, his mouth flew open, and his pipe bounced off the desk top, splattering the shiny mahogany with ashes.

"You son of a bitch!" he roared.

"Mr. Marlow, I—"

"You said he was leaving town!"

"That's what he said, yes, sir."

"That's what he said, or that's what you told him?"

"I told him, yes, sir."

Amos pinned him with his little black eyes. "You'd better be damn sure of that, Mr. Petty, or your ass is in a sling!"

Chink waited for the storm to blow over. In the

past eight years he'd learned the tempestuous little man could erupt into a tirade of vile invective without warning, then as suddenly become as meek as a lamb at a coyote wedding.

Amos limped back and forth behind his desk, favoring his left leg, shooting needles of anger at the defenseless deputy. After a couple of minutes, Amos took up a sheet of white paper and raked the ashes off the desk into a blue ceramic ashtray. He refilled his pipe from a leather-bound humidor, and lit it again with the unicorn. He puffed away, calmly exhaling plumes of gray smoke.

"Chink," he said, "do we have anything to worry about?"

Chink relaxed. The storm had passed.

"I don't think so, sir," Petty said, breathing again. "He saw the sign."

That damn sign! Harvey Wilcox was threatened with everything short of castration, but Hilda's sign was still there after three years—paid for with money Amos gave her.

"We've got to do something about that sign!" Amos said.

"We've tried, sir. Wilcox won't budge."

Amos puffed and meditated. "Timberlake, is it?"

"Yes, sir, Jeff Timberlake."

"Where is he staying?"

"Out at Linus's."

"I want to talk to him," Amos said. "See if you can get him to come around tomorrow morning about eleven."

Chink rolled his hat brim uneasily. He wasn't sure it was a good idea for Amos to talk to

Timberlake.

"Yes, sir," Chink said. He paused at the door. "Mr. Marlow, do you want me to be here?"

"No, no. I'll see him alone."

Chink nodded and went out, not pleased with his benefactor's decision.

Amos puffed and blew.

Why was that Timberlake fellow nosing around? Who was he any way?

And the burning question was—what was his interest in Susie McCord?

Amy's Call

Jeff swung by City Hall, hoping to find someone who could tell him whether Zachary Wheeler ever existed, but it was after five and the offices were closed.

When he got to the motel, Linus said, "Phone call," and handed Jeff a scrap of paper with a number scribbled on it.

Jeff checked the note. Who would know he was there? Had he told Amy Kraft? In his room, Jeff dialed the number. He couldn't believe the voice he heard on the other end.

"This is Amy."

Jeff hesitated.

"Hello, this is Amy Kraft."

"Jeff Timberlake."

"Are you driving a red car?"

"I'm afraid so."

"You're getting famous in a hurry."

"How's that?"

"Half the people in town know who you are and why you're here."

"How would they know that?"

"It's a small town. News travels fast. Maybe we should talk."

"We can do that. When and where?"

"I've got a staff meeting here at school in about ten minutes. It should be over by seven. Do you want to pick me up here?"

Jeff was trying to figure out what brought about the change from her earlier go-to-hell attitude.

"Jeff?"

That was an improvement. She had thawed sufficiently to call him by his first name.

"Okay," he said. "I'll be there at seven."

The Hangout

The City Hall clock struck seven times as Amy settled into the Corvette and closed the door.

"So, this is the famous red car the whole town is talking about," she said.

Jeff shook his head, incredulous. "In living color."

"I've been thinking about you," she said, "since we talked this afternoon."

"It must have been a pretty dull meeting, if that's all you had to think about."

He shifted gears and steered the car onto the street. "So, what were you thinking?"

"About you and Susie."

"Yeah? How did you know where to find me?"

She rolled her eyes. "How long have you been in

town?"

"Since about one o'clock."

"You were spotted as an alien the minute you turned onto Main Street."

"That's unbelievable."

"Believe it," Amy said. "Strangers and red cars get noticed in a hurry. Do you know anybody in town?"

"Not a soul."

"Then I guess it's up to me to show you the hot spots of our city."

"Hot spots?"

"There are only two, one on each end of town."

"Yeah?"

"You have a choice of the Bummer's Den or the Hangout."

"What's the Hangout?"

"It's a beer joint like the Bummer's Den, except it has a live band three nights a week."

"And this is one of the nights?" Jeff said.

"You got it."

"Let's hit the Hangout." He stepped on the gas. "You said you were thinking about me during your meeting."

"I couldn't help wondering why you're so wrapped up in this Susie thing," she said. "Most people put all that behind them long ago."

"Do they no longer care what happened to her?"

"It's not that they don't care. It's just— Turn left here."

"This is the Hangout?"

"The one and only."

The Hangout was jammed with good time

revelers, dancing, laughing, drinking, and loud talk. On a stage against the back wall, a six-piece country band was rocking the foundation with "The Most Fun I Ever Had Was Loving You." A slender, brown-haired woman with large round eyes was cradling a microphone in both hands, gyrating with the beat, belting out the lyrics.

Jeff and Amy squeezed into chairs at a table hardly bigger than Chink Petty's hat.

"Who is that?" Jeff said.

"Who is who?" Amy said.

"That girl. The singer."

"That's no girl," Amy quipped. "That's Jackie Marlow."

Jeff ordered beers from the blond waitress with leather thongs dangling from her thigh-high cowgirl outfit.

"Is Jackie related to Amos Marlow?" Jeff said.

"She's his daughter. How did you know about Amos?"

"Sally Hargis let it slip. And that Linus guy at the motel said everybody pays Amos rent."

"You've got that right."

In her blue denim skirt and jacket, Amy blended well with the western-clad patrons. Jeff, in cordovan wingtips, slacks and no hat, stood out like the red light on Main Street.

That was how Jackie picked him out of the crowd. When she finished her song, she said into the microphone, "Hey, Amy, who's that handsome stranger you've got there?"

The crowd craned its neck to see who the handsome stranger was. Amy covered her embarrassed smile with both hands.

"That's not that red Corvette guy, is it, Amy?" Jackie said, beaming. To Jeff, she said, "You come see me, darlin', and I'll give you something to remember me by."

A chuckle rippled around the room.

Jeff flashed Jackie the okay sign.

"Here's a song just for you, darlin'," Jackie said, sneaking into "If I Didn't Love You So I'd Still Be Gone."

"Well," Amy said, "I guess you won't have to worry about a place to sleep tonight."

Jeff thought Jackie was a pretty talented lady. Some professional singers whose records he'd played on the radio weren't as good. He wondered how Jackie got bogged down in a blue-collar joint like the Hangout in Marlow, Missouri. He'd find out when he visited the Marlow mansion tomorrow morning.

Amy said, "After the way I acted before, you probably wonder why I called you."

"The thought did cross my mind," Jeff said.

She leaned across the table to make herself heard. "Sometimes my kids at school tell me things without knowing they told me," Amy said. "After you left I heard something that sounded like trouble. "I thought you didn't deserve to be hurt. I wanted you to know." She looked around, afraid of being overheard. "The kids say someone is out to get you."

Jeff drew back with a puzzled look.

"Get me?" he said. "Why would anyone want to get me?"

"Two reasons: Susie McCord and your red car."

"That doesn't make any sense. They don't even know me."

"It doesn't have to make sense, and they don't have to know you. Like I said, they know who you are and why you're here. That's reason enough."

"A couple of hours ago you told me to go to hell," Jeff said. "Now it's like you're trying to rescue me from a burning building. Why?"

"Because if the truth about Susie's death gets out, a lot of hard-working people will be hurt. The mills could shut down on a moment's notice, and hundreds of people would be thrown out of work. For four years they've looked for the same answers you're after now, but they still wouldn't take it kindly if some stranger took food out of their kids' mouths if the mills closed."

"What is the truth about Susie's death?" he said.

"Don't ask."

"You think I should forget it?"

"Hell! You're a big boy. What you do is your own business. I just thought you'd like to know what you're up against in this town."

"Thank you."

"You're welcome. Why should I care one way or the other?"

'"Maybe you shouldn't."

"Right! Maybe I shouldn't."

She grabbed her purse and got up to leave. "Don't say I didn't warn you."

"I won't."

She leaned over with her face close to his. "Look—I wasn't born here either, so that makes me an outsider too," she said. "But I don't drive a red car, and I've learned not to talk about Susie McCord." Again she took a look around. "Listen, those kids of mine don't miss much. When I hear something from them, my ears perk up, and I thought you needed to know."

He caught her hand.

She glared at him, her cheeks red with anger. Anger at "them" because of the way things were, anger at him because he didn't take her seriously.

Jeff held her hand until she eased back into the chair.

"So, what do you suggest?" he said.

"Are you going to keep hanging around?"

"Yes."

"You guys!" she said, with a toss of her blond head. "Always gotta be the big hero."

Jeff cast her a tolerant smile and wondered if that was what she really thought—that because he wasn't ready to give up on the Susie case he'd be a hero.

She couldn't know who he was, but he knew.

Jeff was no hero, and had no plans for becoming one.

Most of what he did in his life was to satisfy his personal whims, responsible to no one, except himself. Even so, though Amy had warned him of the possible consequences of pursuing the truth of how Susie died, he couldn't turn his back on her. No one else was taking Susie's part. A young girl deserved better. Even a dead young girl.

"Maybe sometime I can explain it to you," he said.

Amy shrugged as if she understood. "Okay, now, the first thing we have to do is get you out of that flea trap of a motel."

"We can do that. Then what?"

"I've got a spare room at my place. You can bunk in with me for a couple of days."

To his questioning look, she said, "It's okay. My roommate's on vacation."

Jeff hesitated.

"Don't worry about it," she said. "If you'd rather see Linus's face in the morning that's your problem."

Jeff felt a heavy hand on his shoulder. The hand belonged to Chink Petty. Jeff looked up and saw him looking down at him.

Petty was not smiling. He greeted Amy with a nod. To Jeff, he said, "Mr. Timberlake, we need to talk."

Jeff shrugged at Amy, stood up, and followed Chink to a door marked "Office." Chink stepped aside and let Jeff enter first. Petty caught Amy's eye, went into the office, and closed the door.

Amy stared at the door Chink closed. Already the vultures were nibbling at the prey.

Jackie and the band ripped into "Rocky Top."

CHAPTER 8

Hello, Jackie

Jackie Marlow was thirty-nine years old, going on sixteen, some said. She grew up performing in school plays, and singing in the choir of the Presbyterian Church founded by her great grandfather. To be a professional singer was her ambition from childhood. Amos vetoed it as not dignified enough for a Marlow. Jackie considered attending the Chicago Art Institute, but her father said that was too far from home. Once, she inquired about the St. Luke's nursing school in Kansas City. Her father deplored the thought of "my little girl playing nursemaid to some smelly, drooling old codger in a wheelchair."

Jackie, drained of ambition, and weary of fighting for approval, yielded to the lure of alcohol. She became pregnant, and gave birth to a son whose father never saw him.

In recent years, defying the wishes of her father, she unleashed her smoldering desire to follow her dream. "He doesn't like what I do anyway," she reasoned, "so, I may as well do what I want."

The band at the Hangout welcomed her as a kindred soul. They might have rejected her as a rich kid on a lark, throwing her weight around because her old man owned the town, but they didn't, and she didn't. They accepted her as one with the same need as they: To sing her song. And she did it well, losing herself in the music she loved. She handled lyrics like the pro and she never missed a beat. She slurred nary a syllable, even after consuming glasses of bourbon fans placed at her feet on the bandstand.

Jackie sometimes woke up in bed with a man she met the night before. Some people, Dottie among them, dubbed Jackie "the village punch board." Jackie didn't deny it, and seemed at times to relish the notoriety.

In bed with a strange man was where her son Randy found her the night Susie died. Randy was seventeen, the same age as Susie. He ran into the house, frantic with fear, burning to tell his mother what happened at the bridge.

Randy burst into her upstairs bedroom and found her wrapped in the arms of a man he didn't know. He stormed out of the room and banged the door shut behind him. Tears streamed down his cheeks.

Jackie swept up a robe to cover her naked body and followed him down the stairs.

"I know where you're going," she said, grabbing

his arm. "You always run to her when something goes wrong."

Randy twisted free.

"You stay away from that little tramp!" Jackie said.

Randy wanted to scream that "little tramp" fell into the river and he couldn't find her. He wanted his mother to take him in her arms and hold him and assure him that Susie was going to be all right.

"How does that make her different from you?" he said.

"Randy!"

"Don't yell at me, mom. I'm not a kid anymore."

"Then, what are you, Randy? Tell me what you are."

"You think I don't know what goes on up there in that room with those guys?"

She slapped him across the mouth. "You don't talk that way to your mother!"

Randy grimaced, touched a hand to his bleeding mouth, and ran out of the house.

"Randy!" Jackie wiped a tear from the corner of her eye. She had never laid a hand on her son before. "Oh, Randy," she cried.

At The Hangout she could put aside such unpleasantness. On stage with the music she loved, she earned the respect of her fellow performers, and found some for herself.

She finished her song, smiled, acknowledged the applause with a brief "thank you", and saw Jeff resume his seat at the table with Amy.

"What was that all about?" Amy said.

"You know, Amy," Jeff said, "there's something

really weird going on here. Amos Marlow wants to see me tomorrow morning at eleven. Who is Amos Marlow?"

Amy fell silent, escaping to some secret place to be alone with her thoughts.

"Let's go home," she said. "It's talking time."

Hack is Back

Hack Peebles flipped the cap off a Nehi orange and tossed the bottle to Jason Wells. It was closing time at the Texaco. Hack had some time to fool around with his friend.

Jason was white and sixteen, two years younger than Hack. They grew up together on the sand lots of Old Town on the "other side" of the Bois D'Arc River. In the summertime they camped out overnight along the river banks, and hauled in catfish from its waters. They also carried the secret of what happened on the Bois D'Arc River bridge the night Susie died. For four years they told no one what they saw.

Now, here came this guy in the red Corvette, asking questions about Susie, and they decided it was time they broke their silence. Hack chugged a bottle of root beer, and wiped a sleeve across his mouth. His deep sigh and noisy burp let Jason know how good that root beer tasted going down.

"You gonna tell?" Jason said.

"I don't know, man. You?"

"My daddy's been working at that mill since before I was born."

"Mine too."

They fell silent, swigging and thinking.

"It's been a long time," Jason said.

"Yeah. Who's gonna believe what a black kid says about what some white boy did four years ago?"

"I'm not black."

"No, but you're everything else," Hack said with a grin. "You poor, you trashy, and you ugly just like me."

They traded jabs in the ribs and had a good laugh about that.

Jason upended his bottle, swallowed a time or two, and the orange disappeared. "You think Miz Amy would believe us?"

"Yeah, I think Miz Amy would. And that guy in the red Corvette."

"You think so?"

"Yeah, I think so. Didn't I just tell you?"

"Okay. How about tomorrow morning at school?"

"I'll be there."

"See you, Hack."

"See you, Jase."

Amy Tells All

In Marlow, Missouri, the life of a secret was about as long as it took to tell it. Everybody in town knew most everybody in town and a defenseless secret died early. Amy Kraft had heard them all. The secrets, the rumors, the speculation about what happened to Susie McCord.

It was no secret that Randy Marlow picked Susie

up at Dottie's at closing time that Saturday night and took her to a party. After the party, Randy said, he was taking Susie home when she leaped out of his car and ran to the bridge. Beyond that, he claimed to remember nothing. The question in the minds of the locals was, what happened on the bridge? They rumbled in private. Whatever it was, being Amos Marlow's grandson improved Randy's chances of being found not guilty.

It came as no surprise when County Attorney Blake Baldwin decreed that "the death of Susie McCord was by accidental drowning.

Case closed.

The following November, Baldwin was elected to Congress, largely, many scoffed, on the strength of Amos Marlow's contribution to his war chest.

Bryer printed the story of Baldwin's successful bid for a seat in Congress, but was denied the journalistic privilege of publishing an account of Susie's death. Had Mason published any part of the story, the front page of The Voice would have screamed the names of Randy and Amos Marlow, incurring the wrath of the little old man with the twitching goatee.

"So, now," said Amy to Jeff, "you know as much as I do about Susie McCord and what happened to her."

She went to the kitchen and came back with two bottles of Bud. She handed one to Jeff. The other she took with her to the couch where she sat on her folded bare legs.

"And Randy was the last one to see Susie alive?" Jeff said.

"Yes."

"But he remembers nothing after Susie got out of the car and ran away?"

"That's what he says," Amy said.

"But you don't believe it."

"No."

"Why not?"

"Because I think there's more to it that somebody isn't telling."

"Who?"

"Probably Randy. Maybe Amos. Even Cecil Combs."

"You said Combs was the one who found her body," Jeff said.

"Yes. He found the body, but we don't know what else he might know. Susie's death has hung like a dark cloud over this town for four years. It's like the whole town is walking on eggs, afraid we'll say something to cause old Amos to explode, and the whole town could go up in smoke."

"Literally?"

"It's his town. If he wants to burn it, he can burn it," Amy assured him.

"Dottie doesn't believe Randy either."

"Dottie wouldn't believe a Marlow if he wore sandals and a beard and walked on water."

"Thank you for letting me move in on you," he said.

"You're welcome. I hope Linus won't be too broken up about you not showing up out there to-night."

"He'll get over it. Your bathroom isn't off limits, is it?"

"Of course not."

"I need a shower." He followed her down the hall to the bathroom door.

"There's an extra toothbrush," she said, laying out a towel and wash cloth. "Your room is across the hall."

"How about a razor?"

"There's one of those too."

"Thank you again," he said.

"You're welcome again."

He wondered if the razor belonged to her roommate.

Amy turned out the living room light and peered out the front window. She spotted a white Ford cruiser parked at the curb in front of her house with a bank of flashing lights.

"Does he never sleep?" she spat.

Jeff Gets a Call

Amy woke with the sun splashing on her face through the window.

She looked in on Jeff and left him snoozing. She pulled on green sweats and white running shoes for her morning run. It was a daily ritual she dared not neglect. Trim as a willow, she feared growing overweight like her mother when Amy was little. Amy ran three miles every morning before school, promising herself that she would never let that happen to her.

At the end of her run, she saw Chink cruising past her house. "Jeez, Louise!" she seethed. When she stopped running, Chink stopped cruising.

"I noticed you had company last night," he said through his rolled-down window.

"Really, Marshal? How would you know that?"

Chink tossed a nod toward her empty driveway. "I wondered what happened to the red car. I thought he might have left town."

"I don't think so." She was surprised that Jeff's car was gone. It was parked in her driveway when she left to run. "He has an appointment this morning at eleven," she said. "You do remember that, don't you, marshal?"

"I remember. I just wanted to be sure he did."

The cruiser spun away.

Amy was still stewing over Petty's spying when she burst through her front door. She ripped off her running shoes and socks, and left them where they fell, then stripped off her sweats and headed for the shower.

Stuck between the shower doors she found a note scrawled on a Kleenex with one of her red lipsticks.

"Had a call," the note said. "See you later, J. PS. How would anybody know I was at your house?"

Amy laughed out loud. That red Corvette stood out like Orval Faubus at an NAACP convention.

Hack and Jason's Secret

Hack Peebles puffed up the hill to the front door of Marlow High with Jason Wells close behind. Hack spotted Amy going in the door and called to her.

"Well, good morning, boys," she said. "Hack, I

thought you graduated."

"Yez'm," Hack said, out of breath. "Miz Amy, can me and Jase talk to you a minute?"

"Jase and I."

"Yez'm. Can we?"

"What's the matter, Jason? Are your parents on your case again?"

"No'm, it ain't that."

"Isn't."

"Yez'm," said Jason. "We gotta talk to you, Miz Amy."

"All right. You boys come around after school and we'll talk."

"We need to talk now," Hack said.

"Well." She glanced at her watch. "I've got a class in twelve minutes." She gave them a long look. "You guys are serious, aren't you?"

"It's pushing stuff, Miz Amy," Jason said.

"Okay, come on back. You'll have to make it fast."

Jeff Checks Out

Jeff swung by the E-Z Rest to pick up his things.

Linus greeted him with a sullen stare, not pleased that Jeff opted for other accommodations last night.

"Yeah," Linus said, when Jeff told him he was checking out. "I heard you stayed someplace else last night."

Jeff, in town less than twenty-four hours, was no longer surprised that his movements were public knowledge. He flicked a corner of his mouth at

Linus, then went to clear out his room. He gave a crisp goodbye salute to the green bedstead, bowed to the tubless bathroom, and made for the exit. Tossing his bag in the back of the Corvette, he was glad to be saying farewell to the E-Z Rest.

The white Fairlane was crawling past. Jeff shook his head in disbelief. He stared back at the deputy, then watched him speed away with his lights flashing.

He parked the Corvette at Dottie's Diner and pushed the door open.

"Well, look what the cat dragged into my place on a bright Friday morning," Dottie said. "Damned if it's not that Timberlake Jeff guy."

"Morning, Dottie," Jeff said, sliding onto a counter stool.

"How about some of those world famous wheat cakes of mine?" she said, pouring his coffee. "They're always better in the morning. And, guess what, hon. I rounded up some of that Rice's sausage you have trouble living without."

"How did you know I'd be back?"

She wiped the counter top with a coffee-stained towel.

Leaning close, she whispered, "You're not the first one to come in here asking about that Susie sign. The others didn't stay long. But you're not gonna quit till you get to the bottom of it, are you?"

She tossed the towel under the counter, and pinned him with a green-eyed stare. "Or until somebody else gets hurt."

"Who can get hurt?"

"I hope it's not you." She brought his hotcakes

and sausage. "I bet people aren't tripping over each other to talk to you about Susie, are they?"

"No. They tell me everything, except who killed her."

"You think somebody killed her?"

"Don't you?"

She didn't answer.

"Even the town marshal doesn't want to talk about it," Jeff said. "All he said was Susie was dead and buried, and warned me not to stay in town too long."

Dottie was surprised. "You talked to Chink?"

"It was more like he talked to me. He let me know not many strangers stay in Marlow, and didn't want me poking around, asking questions about Susie."

"Chink was in here yesterday after you left, trying to find out who owned that red car. I didn't tell him anything." She refilled his coffee cup. "Chink's all right. He's just doing what he's told to do."

"Who's telling him?"

Dottie gave her head a negative shake.

Around a fork full of hotcake and sausage, Jeff said, "Amy Kraft told me Randy Marlow was the last one to see Susie alive."

"Oh, yeah. I heard you spent the night at Amy's."

"Now, the way I figure it, if Randy—"

Dottie spread her hands in a shushing gesture. "The walls have ears," she said in a half whisper. "Susie was a sharp kid, and a good worker. I loved her like she was one of my own daughters. She had lots of friends."

"How about non-friends?"

"None that I know of. I've heard some kids at school were jealous of her, but nothing serious."

"Do you think Randy could have killed her? I don't mean he'd do it on purpose, but say he lost his temper and—"

Dottie turned her back on him. "End of conversation," she said.

Jeff grabbed his check and met her at the cash register. "How do I get to Jackie Marlow's place?" he said.

"Jackie Marlow?"

"She invited me."

"Don't think you're in a class by yourself, hon. Jackie Marlow would invite a skunk if it wore pants."

"Okay. Are you going to tell me how to get there?"

"South on Main till you can't go any farther. It's a big house. If you keep going, you'll run into the front door. You can't miss it."

"Thank you."

"My pleasure."

He left her staring at his back. Jeff liked Dottie. She was honest. And scared. Everybody he talked to was afraid of something.

He drove south on Main Street, pondering Amos's invitation to lunch, curious as to why the man who owned the town made time to talk to him.

Jeff also wanted to find out what Mason Bryer knew about Susie.

It was Bryer's assistant, Sally Hargis, who called

him at Amy's. He hoped The Voice publisher would shed some light on the mystery of Susie McCord.

Good Morning, Jackie

Jeff eased the Corvette into the circle driveway leading to the front door of the Marlow mansion. He marveled at the great expanse of weedless green grass, and the giant oak trees shading the yard. He took a deep breath, and strode to the front door. He pressed a thumb to the bell, and wondered what it would be like inside the Marlow mansion. He'd soon find out.

The huge oak door swung open. In it stood a dark-haired lady in a pale blue silk robe. Jackie's robe fell away from her shapely bare legs, dipping into a deep Vee in front, exposing a tantalizing pink bosom. She invited him in, and stood aside for him to enter the Marlow mansion.

Not long out of bed, Jackie invited Jeff to a wingback chair, facing him from a wine-colored, velvet covered chaise. Her large round eyes flashed past Jeff's, not quite making contact. Her pouting mouth, devoid of makeup, ambled into a lazy grin.

Last night Jeff saw Jackie at the Hangout as a vibrant, carefree performer, radiating personality and talent. Was this sleepy-eyed, cigarette-smoking woman in the blue robe the same one who bounced around on the stage the night before?

"You don't like me, do you?" Jackie said drowsily, exhaling a cloud of cigarette smoke.

"Why would I not like you?" Jeff replied.

"I can tell. Even last night I could tell."

"I don't know what you saw last night, but you must have misread it."

"Most people think I'm some kind of sleaze bag with no morals."

"Why is that?"

"You must have heard," she said with a crooked grin. "I'm the village whore."

"No, I haven't heard."

She mashed the cigarette into a gold ashtray beside a bottle of Jack Daniel's on a table at her elbow. She grabbed the bottle, poured some into a glass, and sipped at it while she talked.

She held up the glass, inviting him to join her. Jeff declined. It was too early in the day for alcohol.

"I don't give a damn what they think," Jackie said. "Most of them think what my daddy tells them to anyway."

"Is that so?"

"Yes, that's so. He owns everything in town, including the local cop. He ought to. Daddy has paid his salary forever. Chink wouldn't scratch his ass without asking Daddy if it was all right. He owns Chink like he owns everything else around here."

Jeff reflected on Petty's "Don't stay too long." Did Chink deliver an ultimatum from Amos Marlow?

"I bet he doesn't own you," Jeff said to Jackie.

Her dark eyes flashed. She laughed then, reflecting what Jeff suspected was bitterness toward her father.

"He owns me all right, I try not to think about it, but it's true. He dotes on my son. Randy is my meal ticket. Without him, Daddy would have booted me out long ago." She lit another cigarette. "I'm a disappointment to my father," she said. "Here I am, thirty-nine years old, and still trying to find some way to please him." She puffed on the cigarette and sipped at the drink. What did you think of my singing?"

"You're a good singer. I've played records on the radio that weren't as good."

"You're a DJ?" she said, excited.

"I have been."

Jackie drew her robe closer, covering the pink mounds and bare legs. She sat up straight, fussing with her hair.

"Does Randy's father live in Marlow?" Jeff said.

"Randy's father?" She was surprised that he asked. "No, he doesn't live in Marlow."

Jeff got the idea Randy's father she'd rather not talk about.

"He has never seen Randy," she said, "though he tried once."

She leaned forward, and looked squarely into Jeff's eyes, as if about to reveal some family secret.

She was.

What ignited the heated disagreement between herself and her father, Jackie couldn't recall. She was eighteen years old at the time. She remembered running from the house in tears, climbing into her Thunderbird, and screeching out onto Main Street. She didn't recall whether it was by choice or coincidence, but for whatever reason, the Bummer's Den on the edge of town caught her eye. She skidded the Thunderbird to a stop and sat for a while, trying to decide whether she should go inside where she never was before. Her father demeaned alcohol as "the bane of the human race!"

Never had it touched her lips. Some of her friends talked about "getting stewed." Jackie wondered what it would be like, but dared not risk the wrath of her father to find out. Now, though, she needed something to soften the distress of the clash with her father. She decided "a stiff one" might help.

She eased open the door of the Bummer's Den, and stepped inside. The boisterous gathering fell silent. Staring eyes questioned why a Marlow would stoop so low as to mingle with the common folk.

Al Skokie was behind the bar. "Evening, Miss Marlow," he said.

Jackie surveyed the skeptic faces with eyes focused on her. She took a deep breath, dug into her purse, and came out with a dollar bill. She handed it to Skokie.

"Would you change that for me, please?" she said. "Quarters, if you don't mind."

Al obliged, and Jackie strode to the jukebox. She punched in the quarters and selected a dollar's worth of records. They included "San Antonio Rose" and "Steel Guitar Rag" by Bob Wills and the Texas Playboys, and Roy Acuff's "Wabash Cannonball."

The sound of the Playboys' whining fiddles filled the room. Jackie marched to the bar and said to Skokie, "I'd like a drink, please."

Al knew she was underage. He tossed a questioning glance at Jimmy Wiggins, the city attorney, seated at a nearby table. Wiggins nodded.

"What'll it be, Miss Marlow?" Al said.

Jackie remembered two things from when people in the movies ordered drinks: The "usual," and "old fashioned." She didn't know what either of them meant. The usual would not impress Al because he never served her a drink. What an old fashioned was she had no notion, but it sounded more cosmopolitan.

"Could I have an old fashioned, please?" she said

"Absolutely," said Al.

Al turned away, opened a couple of bottles, sprinkled bitters and sweet syrup into a glass of brandy, then set the glass on the bar in front of her.

Jackie took a tentative sip, and then another.

A cheer went up from the crowd, drowning out "San Antonio Rose." A Marlow showed herself to be no better than they were. They went back to their drinks and conversation.

Jackie kept sipping at her glass. Two old fashioneds later, the alcohol began to take effect. Her head was spinning. She wondered if this was how it felt to "get stewed."

Deciding she'd had enough, she dug into her purse again and laid some money on the bar.

Al gave her some of it back. With a look at Jimmy Wiggins, he watched Jackie weave unsteadily to-ward the exit.

Wiggins gave his head a dubious shake, but said nothing.

Jackie didn't know in which direction she pointed the Thunderbird. She lost track of time, and couldn't care less. She was feeling no pain, and even some of her sorrow floated away on the euphoric wings of the alcohol.

Somewhere along a country road she never drove before she spotted a huge oak tree that looked like it wouldn't move if she rammed it with the nose of the Thunderbird.

She did, and it didn't.

How long she lay half-conscious in her smashed up car Jackie didn't know. She felt less than alive, but knew she wasn't dead, though she came close enough to dying to find out she didn't want to go the rest of the way. Late at night on a little traveled dirt road, she tried to free herself from the wreckage. Dazed and confused, she fought to stay awake. She prayed that someone would find her. When no one did after several hours, she was ready to give up.

Then, shortly before daybreak, headlights flashed in her face, and she heard a car slow to a stop. Now, she could sleep. And she did.

In a strange room with stark white walls, her eyes worked themselves open. Flat on her back on a narrow bed, her body ached, and her feet felt heavy as lead. The room smelled medeciny, like she heard people describe hospitals, and she wondered if she was in one.

She was.

A stockily built man with a ruddy complexion and dark blue eyes was bending over her. He smiled, and said his name was Charley Ellsworth. He explained that he found her beside the road, extracted her from the wrecked Thunderbird, and brought her to the emergency room at the Lansburg hospital.

Doctors and nurses huddled over her for hours, then wheeled her into this room on a gurney. Ellsworth told her no identification was found, so the hospital people didn't know who she was, nor whom to notify.

Jackie didn't care. Actually, looking back to the argument with her father, and her introduction to old fashioneds, she was glad nobody knew. Recalling the old fashioneds, Jackie remembered where she left her purse with her driver's license and credit cards—on the bar at the Bummer's Den, thankful for her anonymity.

After surgery, she hardly knew who she was. She gave the hospital a name they could neither confirm nor deny. She wanted nobody to know, especially her father. Had he known, he likely would be mad because she made a mess of as simple a thing as dying in her demolished Thunderbird.

During her stay in the hospital, her only visitor was Charley Ellsworth. He traveled for an insurance company and was gone a lot. When he was in town, he came to be with her. When she was released from the hospital, Charley took her to his home, and arranged for someone to care for her until she could manage on her own.

To Jeff, Jackie said, "How could I face my father? I was eighteen years old, and my life was over. Charley was a few years older and divorced for several years, but, after a while, I knew I was in love with him.

"I also knew I was pregnant with his baby."

As the baby grew inside her, she saw less and

less of Charley. His absences became more frequent and longer. Finally, yielding to the need to have someone with her, she broke down and called home.

"Of course, you can come home, dear!" her mother cried. She had worried about her daughter for the months she was away. Her mother warned her that her father would "raise the roof" when he found out she was pregnant.

Her mother was right. A pregnant unwed daughter was more than Amos could stand.

"I guess you could say he disowned me," Jackie said to Jeff. "He made my life miserable with his constant badgering about Charley.

"In spite of my mother's tearful protests, I couldn't take it anymore. I left again and tramped around a while until it was time for Randy to arrive. I couldn't reach Charley, so once again I came home, hoping things would be different."

Because of her mother's pleading, Amos allowed Jackie to stay. Until Randy was born, few words passed between them.

"Once he saw my baby, Daddy couldn't let him go," Jackie said. "He even threatened if I tried to take Randy away, he would make sure I never saw him again."

Her lips curled into a wan smile. "I bet you wonder why I'm baring my soul to you."

"That's okay," Jeff said.

"My father and I rarely talk any more. Randy is away at school, and with his friends much of the time when he's home. You seemed like someone who'd be interested in what I had to say. I'm sorry if I bored you with my rambling."

"Not at all."

"My father refuses to believe that Randy had anything to do with Susie McCord's death. To believe it would shatter the little world insulating him from reality. But he's still not sure Randy was not involved, and he's afraid if the truth came out, the precious Marlow name would be tarnished."

She strode to the picture window overlooking an expansive lawn shaded by huge maple trees. A small stream gurgled its way across the back yard. "My father and I differ on that," she said, peering out the window. "He's afraid Randy had some-thing to do with Susie's death, and I know he didn't. That's why you're here, isn't it?" Again she faced Jeff. "To talk about Susie?"

"Yes," Jeff said. "I understand Randy was the last person to see Susie alive. I'd like to know what he told you about what happened out there."

"Why? I've heard you're a news reporter, but why would anyone outside Marlow care about a girl who died four years ago."

"The circumstances are suspect. The local paper didn't print the story and has no record of Susie's death. And the people in town don't want to talk about it. I thought you might tell me why."

Jackie took a moment to think about it.

"Susie's death was devastating to Randy," she said, "as it was to many people. I wasn't one of them. I didn't know her then. I thought she was chasing after Randy. It was only after she died I realized how respected she was.

"Randy and I were having some problems, and I thought he and Susie were spending too much time together. I'm sorry for how I felt."

Again she turned to the big window. All her life she'd lived in that house surrounded by its lush green lawn, the giant oak and maple trees, the stream trickling behind the house. How many times, as a young girl, did she scamper up those trees to check on a robin's nest? Were the eggs hatched yet? Searching for colored rocks and tadpoles, giggling at the excitement of wading knee-deep in the stream.

Jeff interrupted her reverie. "Do you and your father talk about this?"

"About Susie?"

Her father was always there. She sensed him peering over her shoulder. Even in school, when she was miles away, she felt his presence, daring her to engage in childish fantasies, to dream anything that she couldn't see or touch. Times when she needed to talk to him, he was too busy.

"No," she said. "We don't talk about it. Not for a long time. It's hard to discuss anything with my father any more. When my mother died, she took much of him with her. Most of the time he's rational. At other times he blames everyone except himself for what goes wrong.

"Six years ago my mother died in a collision with a red truck, and my father was left with one leg shorter than the other. To him it's an imperfection unbecoming a Marlow. He still defiles as evil anything red, especially red cars.

"Sometimes I worry that his mind has left him. He worshiped my mother. Since she's gone, his life is built around Randy. Though he idolizes my son, he never forgave me for getting pregnant with Charley."

Jeff stood up, preparing to go. "You may know, I have an appointment with your father this morning."

"No, I didn't know."

"Marshal Petty delivered the message at the Hangout last night."

"So, that's what he was doing there. You can be sure it's something to do with Susie. My father will want to find out what you know and why you're asking about her."

"Is there anything more you can tell me about Randy and Susie?"

"All I know is what Randy told me. We've had our differences, but I've never known him to lie to me. You could talk to him about it, except that he's back at MU for the fall semester."

"There won't be time for that. I've been advised not to get too attached to your town, and to clear out as soon as possible"

She rolled her eyes. "You don't have to tell me who delivered that message." She walked him to the door. "Much of the mystery surrounding Susie's death is caused by my father's paranoia. He'd move heaven and hell to shield his grandson from any threat of harm." She put out her hand, and Jeff shook it. "I've enjoyed our visit," she said. "Maybe we can do it again sometime."

"I'd like that."

She closed the door behind him, and turned again to the big window. In one of the maple trees, two squirrels chased each other with great leaps and bounds from limb to limb. A blue jay hovered near a nest of little ones, fussing at the squirrels, reminding them of who was in charge. Like her father, she thought. Always in charge. Maybe it was time she had a talk with him. Maybe this time he'd listen.

Jeff sensed the fear Jackie couldn't hide, though she appeared confident of Randy's innocence. With visions of Mason Bryer dancing in his head, he drove away from the big house on Main Street, wondering whether he witnessed a side of Jackie Marlow to which the town closed its eyes.

Jeff Meets Mason

Sally Hargis greeted Jeff with a tight little smile that told him he'd better have a good reason for interrupting her beloved's meditation; else she wouldn't grant him passage to Mason Bryer's private domain. She felt it her calling to throw roadblocks in the path of any who might bring discomfort into the life of the flabby one.

It was Sally who called Jeff at Amy's with a message from Bryer, but that in no way mitigated her dedication to her mission.

Mason Bryer's rocky twenty-seven-year marriage to Beatrice Flow produced two sons and one daughter. After the children grew up and left home, Beatrice, a one-time Las Vegas showgirl, ran away to Arizona with a plumbing salesman she met at a séance.

Beatrice took with her everything she could haul in her 1953 Dodge. The only thing she left behind was a penciled note scrawled on the back of an envelope.

"Goodbye, you slimy bastard."

Mason's sons avoided him. His daughter Rita forbade her kids to go near their abusive grandfather. His kids rejoiced when their irascible father separated himself from the state of California, leaving them free to structure their own lives. Not one of them visited him, sent a Christmas card, nor made a phone call for his birthday in the four years since he left.

Every year on the anniversary of his departure, the kids converged on one home or another, inviting friends and neighbors to help celebrate their emancipation, as the freed slaves must have paid grateful tribute to Abraham Lincoln.

Since time began, some women are fascinated by the crude behavior of sons of bitches. Magnetized by their coarse habits, the stench of their sweaty bodies, and instincts for which animals kill, such women worship such men at their shrines, providing succor and sustenance in times of need.

Sally Hargis was one of those fascinatees. She would gleefully sacrifice herself on the altar of Mason Bryer, sustained by the deathless hope that one magical day he would recognize her as a living, breathing, compassionate woman creature that could bring to fruition his wildest dreams. Oddly, if upon the face of the earth dwelt a human being to whom Mason displayed a modicum of civility, it was Miss Sally Hargis. For Sally, that was enough. For now. And so it was, as a trumpet fanfare resounded in her shell-shaped ears, Miss Hargis pro-claimed to the waiting Mr. Timberlake, "Mr. Bryer will see you now."

Bryer was sixty-two years old. He also was fat. Jeff noticed that right off. Mason's flabby middle wallowed around over the edge of his desk. Dingy white suspenders anchored a pair of wrinkled brown corduroy pants. Where once there was a shock of brown hair, there now shone only a broad expanse of freckled skin.

Jeff tried to visualize what would happen if Mason stood up. Would all that blubber run down into his shoes and across the floor like an avalanche of molten lava?

Bryer ignored Jeff's extended hand, and roared in a voice that sounded like Edgar Buchanan with the croup, "I don't give a good country shit who the hell you are! If you've got something that'll help bring this Susie McCord thing to a head, I want to hear it, and by god now!"

Jeff blinked.

Bryer had more to say. "What the hell do you think you're going to dig up that I don't already know?"

"Is this why you called me here?" Jeff said.

"What?" Mason couldn't remember the last time anyone challenged him.

Jeff moved to the door, on his way out. "I think we're wasting each other's time," he said.

"What—here now!" Bryer sputtered.

With amazing agility for a man of his obese proportions, Bryer joggled out from behind his desk. No lard flowed, as if by some chemical process known only to Mother Nature, the fat did not coagulate around his ankles.

Jeff braced himself as if about to be attacked, certain that in hand-to-hand combat he would be no match for this raging walrus.

"Now, hold on there dammit!" the walrus roared. He pointed a stubby finger at Jeff, his jowls quivering. "Who the hell do you think you are?" Bryer bellowed, "Some big city newspaper hotshot blowing in here, thinking we simple country folks will fall on our faces and lick your boots and kiss your ass because you came to town?" Mason waggled a finger in the vicinity of Jeff's nose. "Let me straighten you out on one thing, mister. I've been sitting on this thing for four long years, and—"

Jeff threw the door open. "Straighten out somebody else," he said. "I'm leaving."

"Hold on there!" Mason screamed. "Don't you walk out on me!"

Jeff whizzed past Miss Hargis's desk so fast he hardly noticed the shocked look on her face.

"Sally!"

She dashed to Bryer's office door and pushed it open. "Yes, Mr. Bryer?"

Mason mopped his sweating brow with a limp white handkerchief. "See if you can get him back here," he said with the sound of surrender. "We need to talk."

Sally sprinted to the front door, and got there in time to see Jeff drive away.

So, You're Amos Marlow

From his office window overlooking the square,

Amos checked the clock mounted below the bronze statue of his grandfather in the City Hall tower. In two minutes that Timberlake fellow would be sprawled on the cushy chair on the other side of his mahogany desk, smirking, stirring up the town again about Randy and Susie McCord.

Amos didn't share his daughter's assurance that Randy had nothing to do with Susie's death. Blake Baldwin pronounced it "accidental drowning," but even Amos questioned the truth of Baldwin's declaration. What if Baldwin was influenced by the fact that Amos was the largest contributor to his political coffers? Would that be reason enough for the county attorney to arrive at a favorable conclusion regarding the guilt or innocence of Randy Marlow?

Amos didn't know—and cared little—whether Baldwin yielded to the temptation to salve the palm of Amos's green-backed hand. The county attorney cleared Randy of any involvement in the death of Susie McCord. Even so, Amos pondered whether Baldwin's action was a payback for Amos's favors. He still struggled with the possibility that his grandson was implicated in Susie's death. That nagged at his conscience, and disturbed his slumber. And, though he struggled with denial, he knew the suspicion of Randy's guilt was alive and well among the local citizenry.

"Young kids drinking, carousing around at wild parties," Amos counseled himself. "No telling what they might get into."

Now, along comes this Timberlake fellow, asking questions, poking his nose into places sealed four years ago. What if he should stumble onto something involving Randy in spite of Baldwin's declaration?

Amos couldn't bear the shame of his name being dragged through the mud, with mitigating head-lines screaming at him from the front page of The Voice, and no telling where else, stripping the Marlow name of its pristine mantle. That much he knew. It was what he didn't know that fed the flames of fear. At whatever cost, he must insulate the Marlow myth from being unmasked.

Amos knew how he was going to deal with Jeff Timberlake. Last night he hardly slept, outlining his plan of action. The best approach was to get right down to it. Let the rubber hit the road!

"What do you want, Mr. Timberlake?" would be his first question. Hit him where it hurts. Make him commit himself, admit that all he wanted was money! Amos never saw a problem that couldn't be solved with money.

Everybody wanted something, especially those young Turks determined to take over the world with no regard for tradition, dedicated to stripping power and influence from people born to it.

Everybody had a price.

"What is your price, Timberlake?" he would challenge. "How much would it take for you to crawl in-to that despicable red abomination of yours and haul ass out of our God-fearing city and never show your face around here again? How much!" Spread a little money around. Frustration, animosity, even sorrow had its limits when soothed by an application of greenbacks.

When Susie's father Dan died of lung cancer from years of inhaling dust in Amos's grain mill, Amos dispatched Waldo with an envelope bulging with money, convinced it would solve the pain of Hilda's and Susie's loss of their husband and father.

Again, the day Susie was buried beside her father, Amos assured Hilda she need not worry about money. He dumped a bag full in her lap. Hilda wondered whether his generosity was a sincere gift of charity, or salve for a guilty conscience. In either case, had he been there that Sunday morning when Cecil Combs came trudging up the hill, bearing to Hilda's front door the lifeless body of her only child, Amos would know that no amount of money could heal the wound of her loss.

Nor did Amos know that Hilda, alone in her grief, cried for three days willing that Susie return to life, even as she went about preparing herself for life without her.

Jackie expressed concern for her father's paranoia, and even some of Amos's closest associates re-marked, "the little old guy seems to be slipping over the edge." More and more, his behavior reflected suspicion and distrust of those with whom he did business for many years.

Amos's head jerked around at the sound of the blaring music from the big clock in the City Hall tower. It told him the eleven o'clock hour had arrived. Jeff Timberlake had not.

Amos grabbed up the phone, and screamed into it, "Mr. Petty, did you deliver my message?"

"Yes, sir, I did."

"Well, where the hell is he?"

Chink peered out his office window. The Voice office was directly in his line of vision.

"His car was parked in front of the newspaper office a while ago," Chink said. "I don't see it there now."

"That Bryer has probably filled him full of all kinds of shit by now!"

"I wouldn't be surprised, sir. Mason's good at that."

"You make sure that boy shows up here, Mr. Petty. Do you understand me?"

"Yes, sir."

Amos slammed the phone down, and looked up sharply in response to a rap on his office door. Eleanor Skaggs, his secretary, eased the door open.

"Mr. Timberlake is here to see you, sir," she said. "Shall I show him in?"

Amos tossed a questioning glance at the phone as though there was some magical connection between his slamming it down and the sudden arrival of Jeff Timberlake.

"Yes," Amos said. "Show him in."

Jeff's conversation with Dottie was prompted by the curiosity of a man in the business of digging for the facts that made news. Her reluctance to talk about Susie, and Linus's fear of retribution, planted the seeds of doubt. They roused in Jeff the determination to uncover the mystery of the sign on the highway and find out what happened to Susie McCord. Petty's implied threat not to stay around too long fired the fuel of Jeff's resolve not to leave town until he was ready.

Why would a man, without provocation, order a

total stranger to "get the hell off my front porch" unless there was something he was afraid to talk about?

What about Sally Hargis and Hack Peebles? How many others would withdraw into their shells at mention of Susie's name? He knew only what Amy told him. Even she was afraid of losing her teaching job if she told what she knew. "Accidental drowning" was too simple an answer. But, if it wasn't accidental, what was it? Why and how did Susie die? Who was responsible for the death of a young girl loved and admired by so many?

Fingers pointed at Randy Marlow, but Jackie was betting her son had nothing to do with it. Did she allow herself to be blinded by the strength of a mother's love?

Maybe Susie fell victim to— What? Jealousy? Vengeance? Subterfuge? Did who she was warrant such sinister terms? The questions kept coming.

How significant must a life be to escape being cut short at seventeen? If it truly was an accident, why all the mystery? Why were people afraid to talk about it? And why was there no record of it in the archives of the local paper? The questions kept popping up, and answers were hidden in the minds of people who believed they knew the answers, but were fearful of retribution.

Jeff expected Bryer to supply some solid information. In his view, Mason was more interested in bolstering his own ego, and feared being perceived as an incompetent ass. The ass part was Jeff's most vivid recollection of his brief encounter with the publisher of The Marlow Voice.

Questions cried out for answers, giving rise to still more questions. What about Cecil Combs? Had anybody verified that all Cecil did was find the body and carry it up the hill to Hilda's house? What did Cecil say when Baldwin asked him to explain what part he played in the tragedy? What about Susie's body being nude when Cecil found it? How did it get that way? Where were her clothes? Where was Cecil now?

Amy told Jeff Chink Petty made the investigation. Chink's findings were corroborated by the county attorney. Susie's death: Accidental drowning. Case closed. Eager as he was to do the bidding of Amos Marlow, townspeople asked themselves how far Chink would go to conceal evidence that might incriminate Randy. With how many more questions would Jeff come away from his meeting with Amos?

Mason Bryer once described Amos Marlow as "about as tall as a turtle pecker." Amos stood hardly more than five feet tall, but he emitted an aura of authority with which few people are born, and for which others die. Pale and frail as Amos appeared, Jeff didn't doubt who was in charge in the city of Marlow.

Amos moved around from behind his desk with an obvious limp to his left side. Jeff recognized the limp as "an imperfection unbecoming a Marlow," as Jackie described her father's injury.

Amos gave Jeff's hand a brief shake, then motioned him into a rich brown leather chair.

Jeff sank into it.

Amos sat on a dark blue-fabric-covered sofa

facing his guest. Between them stood a walnut butler's table from which Amos lifted a silver carafe and poured coffee into two white china cups.

"Cream and sugar, Mr. Timberlake?"

"Neither, thanks."

Amos was dapper in a black, double-breasted pinstripe suit, white broadcloth shirt, and a light blue tie. His shoes were shiny black leather, handmade and expensive. Jeff thought he could have seen himself in them.

Amos stirred a spoonful of sugar into his coffee, and lifted the cup to thin lips separating his mustache from his goatee. The goatee quivered as he placed his cup on the table.

"You're new to our town, Mr. Timberlake," Amos said. It was not a question.

"Yes."

"We have a rich heritage in Marlow, which I'm sure you would appreciate if you allowed yourself the time."

"Yes, sir, but I don't have much time. I've been advised to get out of town as soon as possible."

"Yes, of course." Amos evinced no surprise that Jeff reminded him of Chink's ultimatum.

"I understand you have made inquiries into the tragic death of Susie McCord."

Jeff sipped at his coffee.

"I have," he said. "Is that why you invited me here?"

Amos fidgeted. His goatee twitched, and his little black eyes darted away and back a time or two. This young man's demeanor might make this interview more difficult than he anticipated.

DAVID A. ESTES

"I asked you here to clear up a matter to which our town is extremely sensitive," Amos said, stroking his goatee. "Susie was a fine young girl from a good family. Her father Dan died a few years before Susie. He was a foreman at the Marlow grain mill. His death was a painful loss, as was hers. And her mother's, of course."

Jeff nodded as if he understood. "I haven't learned much. Nobody wants to talk about Susie."

"Susie's death stirred a lot of emotions in Marlow. It's hard to understand how something like that could happen to such an outstanding young girl."

"Something like what, sir?" Jeff got a sharp look from little black eyes.

"Why, her drowning, of course," Amos said. "Her body battered as it was against those rocks. Her neck broken."

Yes, sir, Jeff said to himself, dubious, not ready to believe the story this man told himself for four years.

"Four years is a long time," Amos said. "Over time the pain subsides, people start to forget. Then, when someone such as yourself comes along and wants to know what happened and why, old wounds are opened, the pain is revived, and facts become distorted."

"What are the facts, Mr. Marlow?"

"Marshal Petty investigated and determined that Susie's death was by accidental drowning. The county attorney agreed with the findings, and declared the case closed."

"Baldwin is now your congressman, is he not?"

"He is."

Amos's thin mustache competed with his goatee for quivering rights. He was not used to being quizzed as he was by this audacious young newsmen.

"What about your grandson?" Jeff said.

Amos bristled. "What about my grandson?"

"I understand he was with Susie the night she died."

Amos was not comfortable. "He was with Susie the night she died, but I'm convinced he had nothing to do with the death of Susie McCord."

"What convinced you?"

"Why, Petty's investigation, and the county attorney's corroboration."

"Could Baldwin's determination have been influenced by the fact that Randy is your grandson?"

Amos was on the edge of wrath.

Timberlake voiced concerns of his own. Yet, Amos had dared not admit it, even to himself.

"If I thought my grandson had anything to do with the death of that young lady," Amos said with a flash of anger, "I would personally deliver him to the authorities!"

Uh-huh. The authorities being Chink Petty. "Why are the people of Marlow afraid to talk about Susie?"

"The people of Marlow are free to talk about whatever they wish."

"The ones I've talked to appear to be afraid you'll come down on them if they tell what they know?"

Amos's goatee increased the tempo of its nervous twitch as if he was not pleased with where this conversation was going.

"Do you think Randy could have killed Susie?" Jeff asked.

"There is not one shred of evidence on record," Amos said, eyes on fire, "that in any way implicates my grandson in that tragic accident."

"What about off the record?" Jeff said.

"I have no knowledge of—"

"Wouldn't an accidental drowning in a town the size of Marlow be worthy of mention in the local newspaper? Yet, there is no account of it in the archives of the Marlow Voice."

Amos stewed. That damn Mason Bryer! He would stop at nothing to besmirch the name of a Marlow! No telling what other lies he told this man. Amos shifted uneasily on the sofa, crossed and re-crossed his spindly legs, fingered his twitching mustache, and glared at his inquisitive guest.

"There is no account of it because I—because we— It was determined that it was best to put the matter behind us. Why dwell on such an unhappy event?"

Jeff wondered whether the facts of other deaths were so concealed, becoming non-events.

"One thing I've learned," Jeff said, "is that Randy was the last person to see Susie before she died."

"Who told you that?"

"If we could establish that it truly was an accident—"

Amos got to his feet, waving his arms. "You had

better talk to Marshal Petty about that," he said, signaling an end to the interview.

Jeff wasn't finished. He saw fear in the eyes of Amos Marlow, a different kind of fear from the others. They were afraid of Amos. Amos was afraid Randy might be guilty of murder, a disgrace that Amos could not bear.

Uncertainty clouded his reasoning, driving him to spare no means to protect his grandson from the shame of exposure, sparing himself embarrassment in the process.

"Would you tell me, sir," Jeff said, "what Randy told you about that night?"

Amos was through talking. Why go around poking fingers in the eyes of sleeping dogs? He needed time to think. He limped to the desk, took up his pipe, and tamped it full of tobacco from the humidor. This interview wasn't going as he planned. Had he stuck to the game plan, he scolded himself, it might be over by now. He didn't even offer Timberlake money.

Why hadn't he offered him money?

Amos limped back to the sofa and sat down, puffing at his pipe. "What is your interest in this matter, Mr. Timberlake?"

"I'm on assignment for National News Service. When I saw the sign on the highway, I wondered why anybody would advertise a young girl's death."

"Yes, I heard you were some kind of news reporter."

Maybe now was the time for the money. How much would it take to get him out of town, and have done with it? But, there was something different about this one. The others drifted in, asked a few idle questions, and drifted out again, satisfied with the answers they got. The others caused no trouble, but this Timberlake fellow appeared to be launching some kind of crusade. If it wasn't money he was after, what did he want?

Amos squeezed the unicorn's trigger and touched the flame to his pipe. He used the moment trying to decipher the determination he saw in the eyes of his persistent inquisitor. This one had a more intense look than the others. What did he hope to gain? "You're here in no official capacity then?" Amos asked.

"That's correct. But when a girl's death is advertised on a billboard, and the towns people refuse to talk about it, I can't help wondering why. There's something wrong here, Mr. Marlow. I want to find out what it is."

Amos stared at him, puffing at his pipe. "You know I could have you removed from this office, because I am not obligated to tell you any-thing."

"Yes, sir, you could. But that would only make people more suspicious of you, as well as of your grandson, wouldn't it?" Amos's head moved in a silent motion. Jeff was right, and he knew it.

"Would you join me for lunch, Mr. Timberlake?"

Lunch? With Amos Marlow? Why? Jeff was startled by the invitation. But, he could hardly decline, since Amos probably knew more about the Susie McCord case than anyone else. Why not have lunch with the ruler of the empire and, hopefully, find out what he knew?

Amos didn't wait for an answer. He limped to

the desk, pressed the intercom, and said, "Eleanor, order lunch brought in for Mr. Timberlake and me." To Jeff, he said, "And then, sir, I believe a short ride would be in order."

What Do You Know, Cecil?

Chink Petty slumped in a cane-bottomed rocking chair in Cecil's kitchen. He watched Cecil Combs waddle over to the wood-burning stove.

Cecil lifted the lid off a tarnished iron chili pot and helped himself to another bowl of his hot, spicy, homemade delicacy. He dipped a tin cup into the pot, and said, "Want some chili, Chink?"

"I believe not, Cecil, thanks."

"I made it my own self."

Chink knew that, and he might have accepted a bowl, except Zelda warned him—-"there's no telling what he puts in that stuff!"

What Cecil dumped into the big iron pot were tomatoes, ground beef, jalapeño peppers, chili sauce, green onions, 'possum fat, catfish scraps, and whatever else he could scrounge up to fill the pot. Once a week he stirred up a batch of what he called his "special recipe," and let it simmer overnight. When it passed the taste test, Cecil ate on it for days until the tin cup scraped the bottom of the pot, signaling time to brew up another batch.

Cecil put the lid back on the pot and shuffled back to his green overstuffed chair with the stuffing popping out at the corners. He dropped heavily into the chair, careful not to spill any of the chili from the chipped white bowl on the way down.

Chink waited with the patience of one watching water ice over. He knew there would be no conversation until Cecil was ready.

Cecil Combs was sixty-seven years old. He quit working at Amos's sawmill two years before, and since, suffered a severe case of the "do nothings." He lost Ruthie seven years before and promised himself when he quit work, "I'm gonna park on my ass in a chair with a bowl of chili and grow old and fat at the same time." He succeeded at both.

Cecil wrapped his toothless gums around a tablespoon heaped with the steaming brown stuff, profaning teaspoons as too small. "Ain't no man alive can eat hisself enough chili with no damn teaspoon."

Chink pumped a bit more breath into his patience.

So," Cecil said, smacking his purple lips. "You never come plum out here to set and watch me eat, did you, boy?"

Chink cleared his throat. "Uh—Cecil, you remember you told me about carrying Susie's body up to her mama's place that time?"

A spoonful of chili stopped half way to Cecil's mouth. His hand trembled. The spoon plopped into the bowl and splattered the brown stuff onto his lap. Tears clouded his eyes. He wiped them away with a gnarled fist.

"I recollect," he said. "I won't never forget that day, Chink, if I live to be a hundred. 'Course," he said with a sheepish grin, "I wasn't so damn fat then and could move around a little better."

"You said you found her body up against a

boulder below the rapids?"

Cecil lowered his chin and regarded Chink with a questioning look.

"You aimin' to doubt what I said, boy?"

"No, sir, but it's been a while. I just wanted to be sure I had the straight of what took place out there."

"It's like it was this mornin'," the old man said. "She was washed up agin them big boulders next to where me and Wiley was a-runnin' our trot lines. "All of a sudden, Wiley says to me, lookee yonder, Cecil. I looked over to where Wiley was a-pointin' and seen her up agin them rocks. I couldn't believe it. I thought these old eyes was a-playin' tricks on me.

"Then Wiley and me, we waded into the water, and there she was. Her eyes was wide open, and her mouth looked like she was a-hollerin' for help, or somethin' or 'nother. It scared the shit outa me when I seen it was Susie."

"With four years to look back on it," Chink said, "are you still satisfied it was an accident?"

"That's what you said it was."

"What I said was what I thought at the time," Chink said. "And that's what Blake Baldwin said it was. Not everybody agrees with that, and I want to be sure of what you remember."

"I don't know, Chink," Cecil said with a sad shake of his head. "It was such a sadness for me. That boy— You got to wonder, her neck broke and all."

Cecil waved his hand in a wide gesture, taking in the modest room filled with a collection of odd-piece furniture: An iron bedstead covered with the patchwork quilt "that Hilda made for my birthday." In one corner stood a wooden chest of drawers, its top covered with photographs, some of the red haired, freckle-faced Susie. A tin bread box sat on the cabinet beside the porcelain sink. Mounted over the sink was the well pump with its gooseneck handle. The wood-burning Ben Franklin stove dominated the middle of the room with the chili pot steaming on top of it.

"Susie used to come over here," Cecil said, "and do around for me. She'd straighten things up, wash my clothes, and bring me cookies, or a good hot meal sometimes. Always smiling and carrying on. Just like one of my own, Susie was."

Chink swallowed hard, sharing the old man's hurt. "Somebody's been asking questions about Susie again,"

"Yeah, I heard about that. The feller in the red car. I figgered Amos would be on his case by now. Reckon why he wants to know?"

Chink gave his head a negative shake. "Mr. Marlow is talking to him now. His name is Jeff Timberlake."

"Well, none of them others ever got as far as me."

"This one might."

"If he does, all I can tell him is what I told you, Chink. It won't be nothing different."

Chink stood up and moved toward the door.

"I recollect all of it, Chink," Cecil said. "The look on her mama's face when I come a-carryin' her little girl's dead body up that hill to her front door— That'll stay with me the rest of my life. Somebody needs to be paying for that, Chink. Ain't right nobody never paid for that."

Chink nodded, and turned on a heel.

Cecil waddled out to see him off.

Chink climbed into the cruiser and sped away, squealing tires kicking up gravel as he wheeled out of sight. The cruiser disappeared beyond the weeping willows.

Cecil tore off a jaw full of Day's Work chewing tobacco. The sun filtered through the trees, casting small dancing images on his crusty old face. Orange and red oak leaves littered the ground, and the air hung heavy with the odor of rotting sycamore roots.

Cecil loved it there beside the Bois D'Arc River. That little old frame house was his home for forty-two years, the first thirty-five with Ruthie. Ain't no way he'd ever get over losing Ruthie. Staying in the house she loved helped some.

Cecil turned his face to the open sky.

"Where are you, Ruthie?" he said to a floating cloud. With a break in his voice, he said, "Where are you, girl?" He spat a stream of tobacco juice that formed little craters in the dust at his feet.

"Reckon what old Perk's up to these days?" he muttered.

Jeff Looks Back

Jeff's escape from his father's tyranny after high school opened the path of least resistance to whatever brought him pleasure. Goal setting was an idle pastime in which other people engaged. Ambition went begging, and the only time he worried about money was when he had none.

As a radio personality, he received invitations to share the beds of female listeners whose emotions were stirred by the sensuous resonance of his baritone voice. He made them feel "comfortable," they told him. Rarely did he deny himself the joy of propagating the comfort. He subscribed to the theory that "you only go around once," and devoted an inordinate amount of time to ensuring that he made it all the way around the first time. In his heart of hearts, Jeff felt compelled to satisfy the urgings of as many of the unfulfilled as his time on the planet would allow.

Despite his lackadaisical perception of what a fruitful life would be like, Jeff's natural ability served him well as a broadcaster, a profession perceived by many as a glamorous field of dreams. One of those was Charlene Gore. Jeff and Charlene sometimes consulted each other by phone. They casually touched on "getting together sometime," but never met.

They finally exchanged greetings one Friday afternoon, when media people often got together after work, tipped a few beers and Bloody Marys, and lied to each other about what a fabulous week they had.

From their phone conversations, Jeff envisioned Charlene as a svelte brunette with a come-hither invitation in her baby blue eyes. The woman he met at the party was a plump, twice-divorced forty-year-old with stringy brown hair, eyeglasses as thick as the observation tower telescope, and a Bloody Mary in each hand.

After consuming a few of those, her speech became slurred, punctuated with invectives that would make a Marine DI turn red.

Though his romantic vision of Charlene was shattered, Jeff conceded her ability to sniff out a story was as sharp as an Uncle Milty barb. She earned her job at NNS as a "fearless and tenacious news hound," not because she bedded the boss.

Amos's black chauffeur Waldo guided the sleek black limousine on a tour of the city of Marlow. Jeff wondered briefly how Charlene would have handled his encounter with Amos. Jeff's original notion, when he saw the Susie sign, was to ask a few questions, get some straight answers, and be out of there.

It didn't work that way. He was betrayed by some strange emotion that spawned an obsession with the fate of a young dead girl.

Why did he care? He never cared before. Let it slide. Slap her on the ass, goodbye, and God bless. Except for his dying mother's plea that he deliver her note to Zachary Wheeler, he wouldn't know Susie McCord ever existed. Now he was so engrossed in the mystery of what happened to her he found no place to turn around.

Whatever he thought of Amos Marlow, Jeff couldn't help being impressed sitting next to the emperor of Marlow, Missouri. Luxury of which he knew nothing, except for what he saw in movies. Like Queen Elizabeth riding to Trafalgar Square in her horse-drawn carriage on her birthday, thrilling thousands of spectators lining the streets. Never had he found himself rubbing elbows with royalty such as the emperor of Marlow, Missouri.

Amos's voice yanked him back to reality.

"Right over there," Amos was saying, indicating a small stone building with a Marlow Feed Company sign above the door. "That's where it all began a hundred years ago.

"My grandfather settled this community with nothing but a plow and a mule. He broke the ground, planted the seeds, and harvested the crops. "Because his crops were more bountiful than theirs, other people came to buy his seeds.

"After a while, he gave up farming, and went into the business of developing and selling seeds. After he died, my father followed where my grandfather left off."

Amos leaned past Jeff and waved at a collection of gray metal buildings, grain elevators and storage tanks. "That's the mill. It grew from the little stone building into one of the biggest, most efficient grain operations in the Midwest."

Next came the Marlow Lumber Works from which rose the roar of giant saws ripping oak logs. Smoke poured from the drying kilns, and the pungent odor of fresh sawdust filled the air.

Waldo eased the car past the Marlow Oil Distributing Company, and the Presbyterian Church founded by Amos's grandfather Silas before the Civil War. On the square, Amos directed Jeff's attention to the Bank of Marlow, established by his father Eli in 1893. Atop the City Hall tower, Jeff's eyes were drawn to the imposing twenty-four-foot bronze statue of the stern-faced Silas H. Marlow, gripping the handles of a plow.

The tour was over. Waldo glided the limousine into its private parking space near the front entrance to the Marlow Building—right beside Jeff's red Corvette.

At sight of the Corvette, Amos's chin whiskers began to quiver.

"My father, and his father before him, took care of their own," Amos said. "And I have prospered from their labors, just as the city of Marlow benefits from their foresight and industry. My father cared about the people of Marlow, just as the people now care about each other.

"The death of Susie McCord was a shock to her many friends," Amos went on, "and this entire community cherishes her memory." He concluded his dissertation by saying, "The people of Marlow owe me nothing, Mr. Timberlake."

Uh-huh. Jeff wondered if Amos believed his own words. He thanked him for lunch and the tour, and reached for the door handle. The door was already open. Waldo stood there, flashing a smile. He stepped aside to allow Jeff to pass from the back seat.

Jeff turned toward the Corvette. He paused when he heard Amos call to him.

"Mr. Timberlake," said Amos, still seated in his car.

"Yes?"

Amos decided the crucial moment arrived. It was time for the money, upset with himself for delaying the offer. Did he wait too long?

"How much would it take," Amos said, "for you to stop asking questions about Susie McCord?"

Jeff wasn't sure he heard right. Amos didn't blink. Jeff stared at him. Was the little old man with the piercing black eyes and twitching goatee so fearful of exposure that he was offering him money to let the mystery of Susie McCord stay buried? Did his offer bear the symptoms of what the legal eagles would call a bribe? Coming from Amos Marlow, would anybody care?

"You might want to give that some thought," Amos said.

"I'll do that," Jeff said.

Jeff settled in his Corvette, started the motor, and backed out of the parking place. As he drove away, in the rearview mirror he saw Amos saying something to Waldo.

"You don't like red cars, do you, Waldo?" Amos said.

"No, sir."

"Neither do I."

Waldo read with misgiving the intent in his boss's voice. "Mr. Amos, you don't mean—"

"Spread a little money around if you have to."

"Yes, sir."

Under the windshield wiper on the driver's side Jeff found a folded scrap of yellow note paper. He braked to a stop and grabbed the note. He unfolded it, and found two words scribbled on it. Mason Bryer..

CHAPTER 9

You Drunk Yet, Wiley?

The Bummer's Den stood in the middle of the "Y" on the north end of town where the highway curved east toward St. Louis. The Den was not a world class joint. Julia Child long since scratched it off her list, and Duncan Hines never heard of it. It was the only place in that part of town where a thirsty man could wrap a sweaty hand around an ice cold Bud and relax with his friends.

The front door stood open, inviting any breeze that might lose its way. June bugs bounced off the screen door. From the jukebox, the gravelly voice of Ernest Tabb flooded the neighborhood with "Walking the Floor Over You."

Along one wall stretched an aged wooden bar carved full of names and initials dating back to Jesse James. Four tall vinyl-covered stools stood by for anyone who might have difficulty peering over the bar. Neon-lit beer signs hid holes in the gray plastered walls. The jukebox where Ernest walked was parked near the entrance. Anybody who came in the front door was encouraged to feed it a handful of quarters.

The Bummer's Den also was the only place on the planet where a man could feast his hungry eyes on the luscious Abbie Farr, the bartender. Blond Abbie set many a heart aflutter in her red tights and body-hugging white knit top.

A man didn't always get what he ordered, but nobody cared. Half the fun of being there was watching Abbie bend over to mix a martini or build a burger, exposing a mass of tanned bosom that created a tingle in the innards of goggle-eyed patrons.

Some wag started a round-robin jackpot. Anyone with two dollars could buy a guess at what time on which day Abbie's blouse would explode and her boobs would come bouncing onto the bar. Everybody contributed to the pot. Everybody, that was, except Wiley Hipp. Wiley didn't get excited about women anymore. His pastime was eating and drinking. His habit was parking at a table in the corner by himself. He instructed Abbie to "bring me a couple of ham and cheese on rye. Melt the cheese, please, with lots of pickles and an extra slice of bread." Because he preferred the solitude of his own company, Wiley reminded Abbie, "And don't put nobody else at this table. Okay, Ab?" As a reward for granting his wish, he stuffed a greenback in the deep "V" of her blouse.

Wiley stood five and a half feet tall, and weighed a husky one-sixty, just big enough to qualify for the Marines in what he called "The Big War."

One night on the island of Samoa in the South Pacific, Wiley made a name for himself as a "fearless warrior." Assigned the duty of guarding a gun emplacement, he heard a noise that prompted him to yell, "Halt!" Whoever was out there didn't halt. Wiley yelled again, but the intruder kept coming. A third time Wiley screamed, "You better goddammit halt, or I'll blow your ass off!" The noise came closer, and Wiley, true to his promise, fired a shot from his M-1 rifle at where the noise came from.

The incident gave rise to complaints from island officials. An investigation determined that Wiley blew a hole in the royal belly of a tribal prince who didn't live to tell about it. Wiley's commander shipped him out before daylight. The tribal chieftain was informed Wiley was "disposed of." The chief accepted that as sufficient retribution for the loss of his son, and an international crisis was averted.

Nobody knew how old Wiley was, but he was guessed to be about forty-five.

Since the War, he worked at Amos's feed mill. He also worked his way through three wives and an assortment of other women who told him no. His wives left him for a guitar player, truck driver, and a traveling magazine salesman, in that order. He since preferred eating and drinking alone.

His woman deals took place at the table in the corner of the Bummer's Den. He lived in fear the evil woman fairy might strike again. So, once more he reminded Abbie, "Don't put nobody else at this table."

"Whatever you say, babe," Abbie said, stuffing the greenback between her breasts.

She turned away, but Wiley called her back.

"Yeah, babe?" she said.

"That feller in the red Corvette—"

"Yeah? The one asking about Susie?" she said.

"He been in here yet?"

"No. I heard he was at Dottie's some, but I haven't seen him in here."

Wiley cast her what he thought was a significant look, including a grin that implied that he knew something no one else did.

"Why do you want to know?" Abbie said.

"I just thought he might be looking for me."

Abbie cocked her head to one side. "Looking for you? Why would he be looking for you, babe?"

Wiley crammed his mouth full of ham and cheese on-rye and washed it down with a gulp from the pitcher of beer. With a sneaky grin, he said, "That old boy ain't gonna find out nothing 'bout Susie till he gets to the horse's mouth."

"Oh, okay." Abbie walked away with a whatever shrug.

If it brought the little guy cheer, she'd play his silly game.

Perk's Mission

Perkins Pike was dispatched by Cecil Combs to sniff out the trail of Wiley Hipp.

Waiting by the door of the Bummer's Den, Perk

observed the exchange between Wiley and Abbie. Perk's train had long since jumped the track for, as a young boy, he was kicked in the head by a mule and was not right since. A simple, scraggly-toothed man of forty-nine, Perk's graying hair lopped over his big ears, and his deep-set green eyes never blinked.

On a mission for Cecil, Perk swung by Herb Spencer's barber shop. He idolized Herb as the repository of local lore, and dispenser of truth and wisdom. Perk thought Herb knew everything, and felt an irresistible urge to share with him the significance of his quest.

"Reckon what Cecil wants to see Wiley about, Herb?" Perkins said.

"Beats the shit out of me." Herb was snipping the hair of seven-year-old Bobby Gilmore. To the boy, Herb said, "What do you think, Bobby?"

Bobby squinted while Herb trimmed his bangs. "Beats the shit outa me," Bobby said.

Herb pointed his scissors at Perk. "You never asked Cecil what he wanted?"

"No."

"Cecil and Wiley are big fishing buddies, aren't they?"

"Yeah. Well, I gotta go." Perk was in a sudden hurry to be gone. "I gotta see if I can find old Wiley."

"He's probably up at the Bummer's Den," Herb said. "Wiley spends a lot of time there."

"I reckon I'll go see," Perk said, eager to get away.

"Be sure he's drunk," Herb said. "Wiley's not

worth a cat shitting on a sidewalk if he's
not drunk. Right, Bobby?"

"Shittin' on a sidewalk," Bobby said.

Perk Nniffs the Prey

Perk spotted Wiley parked at his favorite table in the corner.

When Abbie walked away, Herb watched Wiley slugging it out with his frustrated self, downing ham-and-cheese-on-rye, drowning it with guzzles from the glass pitcher.

Wiley didn't like being disturbed when he was eating and drinking.

Perk sidled over that way. From a safe distance he leaned toward Wiley's table, and shouted to be heard above Ernest Tubb walking the floor.

"Uh—Wiley," Perk said.

Wiley didn't look up, and Perk took a cautious step closer. "You drunk yet, Wiley?"

Wiley stuffed his mouth with food, and gulped from the pitcher.

"Who's asking?" he said.

"Perk Pike."

"Hell no, I ain't drunk yet!" Wiley yelled.

Ernest suddenly stopped walking, and Wiley's loud response filled the room.

When he looked up, he caught the glaring eyes of other customers, rebuking him for making a public nuisance of himself with his loud talk.

In a subdued voice, Wiley said to Perk, "No, I ain't drunk yet."

"How long you gonna be?" Perk said.

"Hell, Perk, I don't know. When I'm drunk, I'll be drunk. I ain't much more'n hardly got started yet."

"Cecil said he'd like to talk to you about something."

Wiley showed some interest. "Cecil did?"

"What do you want me to tell him?"

Wiley took a huge bite of ham-and-cheese, and emptied the beer pitcher on top of it.

"You tell old Cece," he said, "as soon as he commences to look as good as Abbie Farr, I'll come a-roaring' out there." He grabbed the empty pitcher, held it aloft, and said, "Do'er again, Ab!"

Back to the Fat Man

Jeff wasn't eager to subject himself to another round of the fat man's verbal abuse, but he was curious to find out why Mason Bryer left the note on his windshield. He hoped he decided to talk about Susie. Or maybe Bryer wanted to dump more garbage on him. On the other hand, if Bryer was ready to share what he knew about the mystery of how and why Susie died, he'd endure the abuse for no longer than it likely would take.

Even so, he decided to let the Voice editor sweat while he swung by Amy's to drop off his things from the E-Z Rest. When he walked into Amy's house the phone rang. With a why-not shrug, Jeff picked it up and said hello.

"Who is this?" a man's voice demanded.

"Who did you call?" Jeff said.

The voice repeated the number.

Jeff checked the base of the phone. "You've got the right number," he said.

"Is Amy there?"

"Amy? No." Jeff didn't like the guy's abrasive attitude. "I think she's in Shanghai."

"Shanghai!"

"Or maybe it's Rio. Could I give her a message?"

"Who the hell are you?"

"Who the hell wants to know?"

"Now, listen—"

"Don't sweat it, buddy, I'm the meter maid. I'll tell Amy you called." He hung up with a satisfied grin. The phone rang again. Jeff picked it up, and said, "Hey, man, I said I'd tell Amy you called."

"Jeff?"

"Amy? Some guy just called for you."

"Oh?"

"I told him you were in Shanghai."

"Shanghai!"

"That's what he said."

"It was probably Alex. He thinks he owns me."

"What do you think?"

"I don't think so," Amy said.

"Is he the roommate you said was on vacation?"

"Let's not talk about Alex. I'm glad I caught you. I've got some news."

"Good or bad?"

"Good. A couple of my kids told me they were at the bridge the night Susie died."

"Your kids?"

"Hack Peebles and Jason Wells. "

"Hack Peebles?"

"He said he talked to you at the gas station."

"He did."

"Jason is Hack's friend. They were camping out near the bridge. They've been afraid to tell anyone about it until now."

"When can I talk to them?" Jeff said.

"Are you staying at my place tonight?"

"Yeah. I just brought my stuff over from the motel."

"Good. We can talk then."

"When will you be there? I've got a couple of things I need to do."

"Sevenish?" she said.

"Save me a seat."

"Bye, Jeff."

"Oh, Amy—"

"Yes?"

"Where could a man buy a billboard in this town?"

"Harvey Wilcox, Wilcox Signs east of the square."

Jeff Finds Harvey

Jeff heard the whine of a siren behind him. In his rearview mirror he saw the white Fairlane with rotating spotlights. "Damn!" he said, giving the steering wheel an irritated rap. He braked to a stop at the curb, and waited for Chink to pull up behind.

Chink unwound from the cruiser, ambled up to the driver's side of the Corvette, and leaned in. "Are you lost?"

"Sort of. I'm looking for—"

"I don't give a damn what you're looking for, man," the marshal said. "You're taking way too much time for whatever it is you came here to do."

"Don't you have anything better to do than ride my ass all over town?"

"Don't wise off with me, Timberlake. I could throw you so far back in my jail that you'd be late for the Second Coming."

"On what charge?"

The marshal answered with a mirthless grin.

"I've got a flash for you, Mr. Petty."

"Yeah? What's that?"

"If I ever decide to break the law in this town, I'll let you know."

Chink didn't flinch. He smiled. It was not the kind of smile Jeff would have wished for, given a choice. It was the kind of smile that said, "You're getting close to the edge, man. Lighten up, or I'll rack your ass."

Jeff said, "Mr. Marlow said I should talk to you about Susie McCord."

Mention of Amos's name struck a nerve, and Petty got interested. He checked his wrist watch. "I'll be in my office in half an hour," he said, turning away. "I'll give you ten minutes."

Wilcox Signs was in a Quonset hut left over from Wiley Hipp's "Big War."

Its half glass front door opened into a small office where two women busied themselves behind a chest high counter. One of them, slender and gray-haired, greeted Jeff with a pleasant smile.

"I'm Jeff Timberlake," he said. "I'd like to talk to Mr. Wilcox about a sign out on the highway."

"Mr. Timberlake? Yes," she said. "If you'll come this way, I'll show you where to find Mr. Wilcox."

She pointed to a door leading to the paint shop behind the office. Wilcox, a husky, pock-faced man of fifty, was seated on a three-legged stool at an easel, drawing heavy black lines on a sheet of white paper. Jeff introduced himself. "The lady up front said I'd find you here."

"Yeah. It's my home away from home."

Jeff wasted no time on idle chatter. "Did you put up that Susie McCord sign out on the highway?"

Wilcox got suspicious. "Are you the one driving that red Corvette?"

Jeff nodded, no longer surprised that his reputation as the red car driver was common knowledge.

"You some kind of cop, or what?" Wilcox said.

"Would it make a difference if I were?"

Wilcox yanked a paint-splotched cloth from a hip pocket and used it to wipe black ink stains off his hands. "If somebody pays me to paint a board, I paint it," he said. "As long as they keep paying for it, it stays up."

"How long has that one been up?"

"Three years."

"Since Susie's mother died?" Jeff asked.

"That's right. The money runs out this month."

"Who paid for it?" Wilcox pinned him with a sharp look, as if he didn't know how far he should go with the conversation.

"I don't know you, man," he said.

"No, you don't. I don't know you either, but I'd

like to know who paid for that sign."

From a white pack with a red circle in the middle, Wilcox shook a Lucky Strike cigarette and lit it with a flip of his Zippo lighter. "Money was left in a trust," he said, not sure he wanted to talk about it.

"Who left it?"

Wilcox blew out a fog of gray smoke that hid his face. "I guess it don't matter now," he said. "It was Susie's mother, Hilda McCord."

"Hilda left enough money to pay for that sign for three years?"

"If I had it to do over," Wilcox said with a nod, "I never would have built it. I've had nothing but grief over that sign ever since I put it up. Twice it was burned down, and twice I built it back."

"Who burned it?"

"I've got my own ideas about that," Wilcox said.

"Do you know how Susie died?"

"Same answer."

"Do you think Susie's death was an accident?"

"Look, mister, I don't know who you are, nor what you're after, but I've had enough grief over that damn sign. I don't know how many times they've threatened to lock me up if I didn't take it down. So far, I've been lucky."

"Who are they?"

Wilcox turned his back, picked up a paint brush, and went back to work.

CHAPTER 10

What Say, Marshal?

The marshal tossed his white Stetson at the wall and watched it land on a wooden peg. He waved at a metal folding chair facing his desk, and Jeff sat on it.

Chink settled into a captain's chair behind the desk, and picked up the phone. "Any messages?" Chink replaced the phone, and eyed the man eying him.

"Before you start firing questions at me," Petty said, "there are some things you need to know." He crossed his boots at the ankles on top of the desk, lit up a Camel, and leaned back in his chair.

"First off," Chink said, pointing the cigarette at Jeff's nose, "I don't have to tell you a damn thing, but since Mr. Marlow put you onto me, I'll oblige.

"Amos Marlow owns this town, Timberlake.

There's a few things around here without his name on them, but it's his town. He probably told you his grandfather started it, and his father built it up.

"During the Depression, Mr. Marlow took care of the rest of us. If the rent came due, or if the kids got sick, and there was no money to pay with, he was right there to help out. In the war years, when food and clothing got scarce, he fixed it so the people didn't have to go without.

"He could have quit a long time ago. He could have closed down the mills, the bank, and everything else and walked away from it free and clear, but he didn't do that. Amos Marlow single-handedly kept this town alive. He made loans he knew wouldn't be repaid. He bought coal and food, shoes for the kids, and blankets with money he never got back.

"Some say he's not the man he once was. We can make allowances for that, because we owe him. Everybody in this town owes Amos Marlow."

Jeff gave that a moment to sink in. "Is that reason enough to slap a gag on the town to protect his grandson?" he asked.

"There's nothing on the record that says Randy Marlow had anything to do with Susie McCord's death."

Uh-huh. Amos told him the same thing. Jeff was within a two-count of testing the marshal's mettle by revealing what Amy told him about Hack and Jason seeing Randy and Susie at the bridge the night she died. He decided he should talk to the boys first. "It's no secret Randy admits being with Susie that night," Jeff said.

"That doesn't make him guilty."

"But, it could mean he was the last one to see her alive. Unless—"

"Unless what?"

"What about Cecil Combs?"

"What about him?"

"Combs found the body," Jeff said. "Maybe he knows more than he's telling."

"Cecil told us his story and we believed him."

"Who do you mean by 'we'?"

"Me and Blake Baldwin," Petty said.

"County Attorney Baldwin, who is now your Congressman?"

"Right."

"What did Combs tell you?"

"Cecil said he and Wiley Hipp were running their trot lines along the river when they spotted a body up against a boulder."

"Who saw it first?"

"Cecil says Wiley saw it first."

"Did Wiley agree with Combs's story?"

Chink swung his boots off the desk, and mashed out his cigarette.

"You're getting mighty damn pushy about something that's none of your business, Timberlake. What are you trying to prove anyway?"

"I'm trying to find out who killed Susie McCord."

"Who killed her? Who said anything about somebody killing her?"

Jeff was getting close, and he knew it. Petty knew it too. Was it time to move in for the kill? "Come on, Marshal, the whole town starts shaking at the mention of Susie's name.

"They're scared half to death Amos will do what you said he didn't do before—close everything down and walk away from it, leaving them high and dry."

"There's no evidence Randy was involved."

"You know damn well he was involved," Jeff said. "You and Amos refuse to believe Randy broke her neck and threw her in the river."

"I don't know that."

"Somebody sure as hell knows that!"

Chink lit another cigarette, and blew out some smoke. "This town buried that girl four years ago, Timberlake," he said. "If you're smart, you'll leave her there."

"Was there no sign of foul play?"

"None."

"Was either Hipp or Combs ever a suspect in the murder?"

"Who said anything about murder?"

"Well, let's look at it this way, marshal. Here's a young girl who has no enemies. Her body is found floating in the river. Her neck is broken, her clothes ripped off, and her body is retrieved by two men who were not suspected of her death. Nobody knows how nor why she got in the water. She was last seen in the company of the grandson of the man who owns the town. The editor of the local newspaper is not allowed to print an account of her death. You're the law in this town, Mr. Petty. Do you see anything suspicious about this picture?"

"You don't know what you're talking about."

"And how do you account for her body being

nude?

"It couldn't have taken more than a few minutes for the current to carry her downstream—not long enough for it to tear off all her clothes. And where are her clothes now?"

"Her clothes were never found," Chink said.

"Her clothes were never found?"

Petty gave him a look that said he was about through talking. Jeff wasn't. "What did Randy say about that?"

"I didn't ask him."

"Would you like me to guess why you never asked the prime suspect whether he ripped Susie's clothes off before he threw her in the river?"

"I didn't think it was necessary at the time."

"So, you don't know whether she got into the river with her clothes on, or if Randy ripped them off, or if—"

"You're out of line, Timberlake."

The deputy who'd been nicknamed 'the marshal' was not comfortable. *Who is this guy anyhow? What does he know about anything? What gives him the right to punch, jab, and blast below the surface of a lawman's conscience?*

For four years Chink asked himself the same questions Timberlake was firing at him now. He didn't look for answers from anyone else because he wasn't sure he wanted to hear what people had to say. He still wasn't sure. It was being brought home to him now, by this stranger, who claimed to be from some news outfit, that he wasn't honest with himself. When his suspicions got too close to Randy, he did an about-face, prompted by his obligation to Amos Marlow. Conscience be damned!

He had to pay rent and feed hungry kids. Chink got to his feet, and tossed a thumb over his right shoulder toward something neither of them could see. "That sign out there says Susie McCord died here. I've come to accept that, Timberlake. The townspeople accept it, and you'd save yourself a hell of a lot of trouble if you'd forget about it and move on."

Jeff got to his feet. It was not yet moving on time. "What kind of trouble?"

"Don't push it, Timberlake."

"Would you push it if Susie hadn't lived on the wrong side of the river?"

Chink checked his watch. "Your time's about up, but there's one more thing you need to understand. If it weren't for the rich man in this town, there wouldn't be anybody else. Amos Marlow provides jobs for most of us, and the town depends on him for a living. Not everybody likes it that way, but that's how it is. Once you get used to it, it don't wash out too bad."

He moved a step closer, and leaned into Jeff's face.

"And it don't have a damn thing to do with which side of the Bois D'Arc River Susie McCord lived on."

Jeff stared back for a moment, then moved to the door. "There's something you need to know too, Mr. Petty. This Susie matter could have been over and done with long ago if the whole town didn't try to hide it. The more I look, the more convinced I am that something rotten is going on here, and I'll leave town after I find out what it is. I've broken no laws. I've done nothing wrong, except ruffle a few feathers that needed ruffling. So, if you're going to lock me up, do it now, or get the hell off my back." He waited for a five count, then left the marshal staring at the door Jeff closed behind him.

"Sundown tomorrow, Timberlake!" he heard Chink yell at his back.

Jeff strode past Lil Barnes's desk. She smiled to herself and kept typing.

Bryer Again

Jeff cooled his heels while Bryer fumed on the phone. He debated with himself whether to tell Mason about Amos's offer of money to forget about Susie. Mason likely would rejoice at the news, eager as he was to nail the little man with the twitching mustache. And what about Hack and Jason? Should he tell Bryer they saw what took place at the bridge that Saturday night?

Considering the foul mood he'd left the fat man in earlier, Jeff wasn't anxious to share anything with him. Why he left that note on his windshield topped Jeff's list of curiosities.

Bryer banged the phone down.

"Son-of-a-bitching political parasite!" he seethed. "Blake Baldwin. He calls every other day demanding a free spread for his run for re-election. He thinks because he's Marlow's man he can throw his weight around and get a free ride. I'll free ride his ass!" Mason raked a beefy hand across his flaming face.

Jeff expected some comment about Bryer's earlier outburst, but Mason charged ahead as though it never happened.

"Baldwin was the prosecuting attorney when Susie died," Bryer said. "He claimed there wasn't enough evidence to pursue the case, and called it good. The son-of-a-bitch was on Marlow's payroll at the time. Still is, I'd guess."

Jeff sat on a chair across from Bryer, and listened while he raged.

"Everybody in town knows that Marlow kid was involved in this thing. He admits being with Susie at the party, but claims he can't remember what took place after Susie left his car and ran to the bridge. Bullshit!"

Bryer huffed around, stalking back and forth behind his desk, swabbing his freckled pate, spouting bad things about Amos Marlow, looking at the floor, formulating his next vindictive blast. Jeff was pretty sure though Bryer wasn't through talking. Mason didn't acknowledge his presence.

"Between Marlow and Baldwin," Bryer went on, "they slapped a gag on the whole town, and everybody's scared shitless to even talk about the death of Susie McCord."

"And you weren't allowed to print the story?" Jeff said.

Mason jerked his head around as if aware for the first time that he was not alone. "Hell no, I didn't print the story! They threatened me with everything up to and including hanging me by the balls from the City Hall tower. You want pictures, police reports—even an obituary? There are none, and there never were any!

"That's what makes me so damn mad. You spend your life hoping someday you'll get a shot at what you've always wanted to do. When you think you've got the chance to get it done, somebody sticks a pitchfork up our ass and dares you walk!

"You see, Timberlake, Baldwin hushed this thing up because Amos paid him off. Petty falls in line because Marlow pays his wages. The town won't do anything but bitch about it to each other because they all owe Amos. And Amos can't afford a court hearing because he's afraid that little bastard is guilty as hell." Bryer sniffed at that, displaying a vengeful smile.

"That would be a blight on the sacred Marlow name. That old fart would keel over dead with a massive attack of the nervous twitches. Amos worships that kid."

At sixty-two, Bryer was a physical embarrassment to Mother Nature. Beer and pizza, Jeff guessed. Beyer didn't fit the mold of what Jeff envisioned of a dignified, in-control newspaper executive. Jeff formed a mental picture of Mason in a pair of Big Smith overalls and a green John Deere base-ball cap, spreading cow manure behind a tractor, or stirring up a cloud of dust in a cornfield.

Even so, in the span of a few minutes, on a scale of one to ten, Jeff's appraisal of the brash Bryer rose to about an eight. Beneath that mass of unruly flab, he thought, dwelt a substance of uncommon character. Bryer wouldn't live long enough to see a monument erected in his honor on the City Hall square, but Jeff believed he deserved a better hand than the city of Marlow dealt him.

"Through a purchasing exchange," Mason was saying, "I had a chance to buy The Voice. I came out here and looked things over, and liked what I saw. The mistake I made was not looking closely enough at the politics.

"I dabbled in writing, sold a few pieces to magazines, and hoped someday to buy a small town newspaper. I thought I would have editorial control, and say what I thought needed to be said." He gave his bald head a sad shake. "I found out I couldn't control shit. Susie died the week I took over the paper.

"Cecil Combs barely showed up on Hilda's doorstep carrying Susie's body before Chink Petty parked his ass on that chair you're sitting on. He told me Susie's death was an accident, and I didn't need to get crossways with the wrong people early in the game. The Bank of Marlow holds the mortgage on the paper. They let me know they'd close me down if I printed the story." Mason wiped his sweaty brow.

Jeff said, "I had lunch with Mr. Marlow."

"Yeah, I wondered when you'd get around to that. I saw your car parked over there."

"You left the note?"

Bryer nodded. "I've been fighting this thing for four years, Timberlake. You pop in here full of spit and vinegar, playing Perry Mason, like you were going to get all the answers in a half hour. I resented that, and I was wrong. You need all the help you can get. So do I. I'd like to bust this thing wide open, and expose Amos Marlow for the phony he is. You and I seem to be the only ones who care about Susie." He dragged an impatient hand across his face and gave Jeff a solemn look. "I'm sure Amos gave you the grand tour."

"He did."

Jeff believed Bryer was genuinely concerned about the mystery of how Susie died. If he couldn't tell Bryer about Amos's money offer, who could he tell?

Making headway toward solving the mystery of Susie McCord, as Mason said, he needed all the help he could get.

"He offered me money," Jeff said.

"Who?"

"Amos Marlow."

Over the tops of his wire-framed eyeglasses, Mason peered at him with a fixed stare. "Say that again."

"Amos Marlow offered me money to stop asking questions about Susie McCord."

"Are you absolutely certain that's what the man said?"

"He said how much would it take."

Bryer bounced to his feet. "Hot damn!" he shouted gleefully. He swept off his glasses and pointed them at Jeff. "Were you and Amos alone at the time he made the offer?"

"The black man was there."

"Waldo. Did he hear Amos say 'how much would it take'?"

"I don't know, but he was as close to me as you are."

Mason paced back and forth behind his desk. His face lit up with a rapturous glow. "Hot damn!" he beamed again. He snapped his suspenders, eyes glistening with excitement. "What's your next move?" he said.

"I'm not sure," Jeff said, "but I think the county attorney should know about this."

Bryer agreed. "Damn right! When this thing broke, Hale Witcher was the assistant prosecutor under Baldwin." He scribbled something on a scrap of paper and handed it to Jeff. "That's Witcher's address. He's now the county attorney, and offices in the courthouse at Lansburg. I've had a few dealings with Witcher. Unless I miss my guess, this bribery thing will give him the ammunition he needs to reopen the Susie case."

Jeff stuck the note in a pocket and got up to go. "I don't have much time," he said. "Petty gave me till sundown tomorrow to wind up whatever I came for."

"What did you come for?"

"A man named Zachary Wheeler. He was a friend of my mother's. She died a few days ago and asked me to deliver a letter to Wheeler."

Bryer shook his head. "The name doesn't ring a bell. He must have been before my time."

"How do I get to Lansburg?" Jeff asked.

"Seventeen miles east. I'll call Witcher and tell him you're on the way." He walked Jeff to the door. "What are you going to do with whatever you find?"

"I'm obligated to a friend at NNS in Des Moines. Aside from that, if you want it, you've got it."

"You bet your sweet ass I want it! You dig it up, and I'll damn well print it."

Jeff nodded to Miss Hargis on his way out. He didn't know Hale Witcher, but he'd soon get acquainted.

Hello, Daddy

Jackie Marlow swept past Eleanor Skaggs's desk and tossed her a tight smile on the way to her father's office.

"Miss Marlow," Eleanor sputtered, "you can't—"

"I know," Jackie said, and kept walking.

She waved off Eleanor's implied threat and burst through the heavy oak door. Amos was on the phone. "Daddy," Jackie said.

Amos covered the phone with a hand, and said, "Can't you see I'm busy?"

She marched around the desk and pressed the disconnect. "We need to talk," she said.

"Jackie! Can't we do this another time?"

With a deep sigh she sank into the big chair recently occupied by Jeff Timberlake. A red wave of irritation flooded her father's face. How many times, growing up, was she put off when she needed to talk to him? The first time she made the honor roll in third grade, she couldn't wait to tell him, and ran all the way home. He dismissed her with, "Can't you see I'm busy?" She turned away with tears in her eyes.

When she was voted football queen at Marlow High he was too busy to escort her onto the field to receive her crown. At eighteen, when she told him she was leaving home to pursue a career, he said, "Do we have to discuss this now?"

She forced a sad smile. "It has always been this way, hasn't it, Daddy?" Jackie said. "You've never quite known what to do with me, have you?"

"What do you mean by that?"

"One of my earliest recollections is of you telling me you didn't have time to talk to me."

"Well, I can't always just drop everything," Amos said.

"You know someone else has been asking questions about Susie."

"Yes, yes, I know about that."

"Do you know what people are saying?"

"What they're saying?"

"About Randy and Susie McCord."

"I've heard about that, but it's nothing to worry about."

"Nothing to worry about?" She was incredulous. "The whole town believes Randy was responsible for Susie's death, and you say it's nothing to worry about?"

"People believe what they want to believe, but they don't know anything. We'll take care of it."

"The same way you took care of Charley, by having him run out of town?" She hadn't meant to say that, but the words erupted like a simmering geyser. For years she needed to say it, since the day Charley came looking for her and their son Randy. Amos wouldn't allow him in the house, afraid Charley might take Randy away, and "took care of it."

"Who? Charley?" Amos said. "That white trash?"

"And what kind of trash are we, Daddy?"

"Now, Jackie, you know—"

"Answer me, Daddy! I want to know. Are we the kind of trash people sweep under the carpet, or hide in a closet, or burn in the alley? Are we the kind of trash that's afraid to face up to the truth because it might reflect on the precious Marlow name?"

"What are you getting at, young lady?"

Startled, she blinked. When was the last time he called her young lady? "What does it sound like?"

"It sounds like you're overstepping the bounds of respect and authority."

"Respect and authority be damned! Is that all we've got left? If those people out there take matters in their own hands, my son's life could be in danger." In her father's eyes Jackie saw something she never saw before. She saw fear.

For four years he denied that Randy killed Susie McCord. His grandson could not be guilty of such a thing. Amos refused to concede, even to himself. Jackie was appalled. Her father was so afraid his grandson killed that girl that he closed all doors that might open to the truth.

"The people?" Amos said. "They won't do anything. All they've got is what I give them. They don't have the courage to do anything about it."

Jackie recognized the symptoms of paranoia, leaving no room in his mind for reality.

She now felt an odd longing to throw her arms around him and hold him close, but did not. He wouldn't understand such a display of emotion, and likely would reject her—again. Her eyes sparkled with tears, like times when she was growing up.

"The anniversary of Susie's death is coming soon," she said, reining in her emotions. "Why don't you call Mason Bryer and tell him to print whatever information he has as a sort of memorial to Susie?"

"No, no, it has been too long. The facts—"

"Tell him he can talk to anyone he wants, and print whatever they tell him."

"I can't do that." Amos was aghast that she would suggest such a thing.

"Let the people know you're not afraid, and they need have no fear of you." Jackie urged. "They'd have a lot more respect for you, and you may be surprised at what good would come of it."

"No, no! You're asking too much!"

"That's the only way we can ever put this behind us, Daddy."

"You don't know what you're asking. It's too hard. I must protect my grandson."

"From what, Daddy? We don't know that he needs protecting. I believe what Randy told me. Susie was alive when she fell into the river."

With an unsteady hand, Amos stroked his trembling goatee. "How can you be sure that Randy was not involved?" he said.

"I'm his mother." She was shocked at the sound of her voice. When did she last utter those words? "I'm his mother!" They echoed off the walls of her mind, affirming with three little words her pride and trust in her son.

"I know my son," she said. "Sure, we've had our

differences, and Randy hasn't always been a model child, but he never lied to me."

"It might be different if he'd had a father."

"He had a father!" she snapped, eyes ablaze. For the first time in her life she challenged her father without fear, as if energized by some alien strength. "But, thanks to you, I have no husband! You're right. Things would be different. Randy would have a father to look up to, but that wouldn't make him any less guilty of Susie's death!"

"Now, Jackie, we don't know that. There was drinking going on at that party, though the Lord knows I've talked to him enough about that.

"Randy might have drunk too much, and he and Susie maybe had words on the bridge. Maybe Randy flew off the handle. You know how he was at that age, worked on a short fuse much of the time."

He tugged at his goatee, his eyes slits of suspicion, speaking in a low voice as if to himself. "That man—that Timberlake fellow. I met with him today to find out what he knew. It didn't amount to much. Just enough to muddy the waters again, and throw the town into an uproar."

Jackie wanted to be gone from the presence of this pitiful little old creature who suddenly became someone she didn't know. Already, in his mind, he convicted her son, committed to shielding Randy from some unidentified disaster. Her father deluded himself that his concern was for Randy.

She now suspected his fear was as much for himself. His obsession was to insulate Amos Marlow against the unbearable scandal of having the family name dragged through the public square, defiling the honor of his bronze grandfather's statue, monitoring his every move from atop the City Hall tower. "Mr. Timberlake came to see me today too," she said.

"Oh? And what did you tell him?"

"Would you be surprised that I told him the truth?"

"I would expect nothing less of you," he said. "I never did."

"Facing the truth is something we haven't done much of lately," Jackie said.

"All I ever wanted was to protect Randy."

Jackie questioned the truth of that, but didn't challenge it. "What are you afraid of?" she asked. "Baldwin said it was an accident. Hiding the truth, whatever it is, reflects on us as much as if we paraded our guilt down the middle of Main Street."

"You never can tell. That Timberlake fellow. If he keeps snooping around—"

"Well, you know, Daddy, someday Randy will have to stand up and find out for himself what kind of man he is. He can't do that as long as you keep building walls around him, shutting him off from reality, and doing everything for him."

"I wouldn't let Randy be hurt for anything in the world," Amos said.

Jackie thought she detected a rare dampness in his eyes. "I know that."

"That boy— He was all your mother ever cared about."

Jackie moved to the door. "I know, Daddy," she said with a sad smile.

"Now, Jackie, you know— Your mama— I didn't mean—"

"Let it go, Daddy. Mama's gone, and that was a long time ago." She closed the door behind her as she left. On her way out, she tossed Eleanor a wan smile. "If he should ask, tell him I've gone to be with my son."

CHAPTER 11

Wiley Answers the Call

Rain clouds hovered over the late afternoon as Wiley Hipp dashed out of the Osage orange grove. He slipped warily into the willows hiding Cecil's house on the dirt road winding along the Bois D'Arc River. He moved stealthily from one tree to the next. Stuffed with ham and cheese on rye, stoked to the gills with Abbie Farr's beer, he was running from the enemy tormenting his alcohol-saturated mind. Haunted by ghosts of the past, Wiley sought refuge on a sand-and-palm-tree speckled island of the South Pacific. He glanced about, turned up his collar against the rain, and made a dash for Cecil's front door.

Wiley took a last frenzied look around with his back to the door, burst through the door, and slammed it shut behind him. Safe at last!

Cecil was so startled by Wiley's noisy entrance he dropped his spoon in the chili bowl and splattered himself with the brown stuff. "Damn, Wiley! What the hell are you doing?"

"Gotta be careful, Cece. You never know who might be coming up behind you."

"Are you still running from that Samoan prince?"

"I can't help it, Cece. I see him all the time."

Cecil poked a chili-loaded spoon between his purple lips. He knew not to offer Wiley any of his "special recipe." The last time he invited Wiley to join him, Cecil recited the list of ingredients, and Wiley threw up in his bowl.

"You reckon I got a devil in me, Cece?" Wiley said.

"Wouldn't surprise me none. Most everybody's got one of some kind. Gambling, whoring, drinking, lying. Don't cow-tow to it and it'll prob'ly go away."

Wiley plopped down on the floor at the feet of the older man, his ankles crossed, elbows folded on his knees. He peered into Cecil's crinkled face as if seeking the wisdom of the village guru. "You got any devils, Cece?"

"Had me a devil once." Cecil's face lit up, and his small round eyes sparkled, recalling pleasures of times past. "She-devil name of Ruthie," he said. "Her and me was married."

"The hell! You never said nothing about no wife. Where's she at now?"

"Dead." Spoon at half mast, eyes bleary. "Ruthie's dead, Wiley."

"Aw, Cece! How'd she die?"

"Some likkered up bastard raped her, broke her neck, and th'owed her in the river."

Wiley's eyes got big with wonder.

"Damn, Cece! What happened to the one that done it?"

"Nothin'. You know, Wiley, if you got a sickness they can't do nothin' to you. They can't even th'ow you in jail."

"I never knowed that."

"Well, they can't. Some shyster lawyer told the judge that old boy had some kind of sickness. The judge said, all right we'll just send him off to the hospital till he gets hisself over it. And that's what they done. They can't do nothin' to you if you got a sickness, even if you rape somebody and break their neck and th'ow 'em in the river."

Cecil's old eyes glazed over and he drifted off to some place where Wiley didn't feel welcome.

The old man sneaked a thumb up to wipe something from the corner of an eye.

"Don't bother me now, Wiley," he said. "I'm a-havin' Ruthie."

Wiley's patience grew thin after a while. "Uh—Cece, Perk said you wanted to talk to me about something or other."

Cecil shook the glaze from his eyes.

"Yeah," he said. "I ain't seen you for a while. I figgered Perk'd know where to look for you."

He squinted into Wiley's hollow-eyed countenance, hoping the little guy would understand what he was about to say.

"Some feller come to town and been nosing

around," Cecil said, "asking questions about Susie."

"That's the one in the red car?"

Cecil nodded. "I figgered you and me better have a little confab about what happened out there in case he looks you up."

Cecil's eyes wandered past Wiley's shoulder to the scarred wooden chiffonier.

He focused on a picture of Susie, freckled as a Dalmatian, red hair flying, green eyes full of laughter. Who'd ever thought she'd wind up dead on them rocks?

"Chink Petty was here a while ago," Cecil said. "He was checkin' up to see if I forgot anything about that night I told him before.

"You ain't forgot nothin', have you, Wiley?"

"I ain't forgot nothin', Cece." Wiley tapped his right temple with a forefinger. "I got it all right up here."

"Are you plum sure of that?"

"I'm plum sure."

Cecil was not. "You drunk bastard," he said with a wide grin. "You don't remember nothin', do you?"

"Don't call me that, Cece. I ain't no drunk bastard."

"The hell you ain't." Cecil laughed out loud. "You ain't nothin' but a drunk, stupid bastard, and drunk, stupid bastards don't remember nothin'."

Wiley was hurt. He and Cecil fished and hunted together for years. They even got drunk together before Cecil suffered a bad case of the DT's and took the cure. What came over Cecil that caused him to ridicule his best friend? Wiley grabbed his hat and stormed out the door. "I'm leavin'."

"Where you going?" Cecil called after him. "Are you all right, Wiley?" The little guy kept going.

Jeff Looks Back

Jeff was concerned that he might not find the man whose name his mother gasped with her dying breath. Whatever happened between her and Wheeler must have been years ago and no longer mattered, except that she was anxious that he "tell Zach about me." Linus said Wheeler once worked for Abe Goldman. How long ago was "once", and what became of Wheeler?

Visions of Leota and Zachary together began taking shape in Jeff's mind. A curious little smile sneaked across his lips as he drove toward Lansburg. Nah. She'd never do that. Even cowed and resentful as she was toward his father, she wouldn't— Would she? His thoughts leaped back to the day when he was eight years old, peering out the living room window, waiting for his mother to come home. Jeff saw her get out of a long black car that stopped in front of their house.

The car pulled away, and a smiling Leota walked to the front door. By the time she got to the door, her smile was gone, and she no longer looked happy. Jeff wondered why, but never asked. Why not? 'The question vaulted to the front of his mind. Like the day a voice inside him shouted, "She's a whore!"

Why not, indeed? Wasn't his mother entitled to some happiness that she didn't find at home? Jeff could recall no time when he witnessed a display of affection between his parents. Nor had there been any between himself and his father. That was a void he tried to forget.

How much forgetting can a man do? And how much remembering is too much? In his growing up years he was frightened by the sight and sounds of people in the grasp of convulsions, reacting to his father's hellfire and damnation sermons. Begging forgiveness for sins yet uncommitted, and vowing allegiance to a God of whom they knew little, except what his father frightened them into believing.

Brother Ethan Timberlake depicted God as dark and menacing, an angry God who rewarded with pain and suffering all who believed in Him. Recalling the fanatical outbursts of his father, who claimed to fear the God he preached about to his congregation, Jeff shuddered. Yes, he told himself, Leota deserved happiness wherever she found it. Even so, it was hard for Jeff to convince himself his mother would be unfaithful even to Ethan, a man whose only passion was his ominous Biblical rhetoric.

Okay, Jeff conceded finally. He would stop by Abe Goldman's Jewelry, have a chat with Leland Haymes, and make an effort to locate Zachary Wheeler.

But that would have to wait. That—whatever happened between Wheeler and his mother—was a long time ago. Susie McCord was now. Susie came first.

Light rain sprinkled his windshield as he stepped on the gas. He hoped Witcher would be in his office when he got there.

He was.

Hale Witcher was the best damn lawyer in Osage County. Ask anybody. Ask that man there in the striped overalls leaning against the post in front of Billy Hooper's hardware store.

"Who's the best damn lawyer in Osage County?"

"Hale Witcher."

See there? Everybody knew, even if you called Blake Baldwin at his Congressman's office in Washington, D. C., he'd tell you the same thing. Baldwin said so even when Witcher was his assistant prosecutor.

The only mistake Witcher ever made that anyone remembered was not marrying Donna Jean Furkin. He could have. Donna Jean was willing, but Hale married that Haverly girl from over around Stockton. Why Hale married Essie instead of Donna Jean was no secret.

Essie was a fine young woman, but nobody believed she was right for Hale. Donna Jean was.

Witcher's marriage to Essie produced two beautiful daughters and one handsome son. But, Hale and Essie amassed a passel of marital problems that never got solved because they were seldom on the same wavelength. Compatibility was alien to the union. For years they nibbled around the edges of divorce. They agreed to stay married until after the kids were up and gone. Meantime, Hale and Essie went their separate ways, pursuing their individual interests.

Donna Jean married Brent Caster. A willowy brunette with brilliant gray eyes and a constant smile, Donna Jean could have any man she wanted—except Hale Witcher. Hale wanted her too, and had for as long as he could remember. Why then, one might ask, did they not marry each other?

Hale and Donna Jean were "practically engaged" since grammar school. Half of Osage County knew that, and expected them to get married someday. They didn't because on the day Hale passed the Bar exam, Donna Jean was touring Europe with her parents.

In the course of celebrating his becoming a bona fide lawyer, Hale and Essie ran into each other at a party. According to eyewitness accounts, they participated in a spate of congratulatory toasts, after which they wound up in the back seat of Hale's old Ford.

And the rest, as they say, was history. Eight months after the wedding, their first daughter arrived. That's how it was done in those times. If the girl became "with child," the boy married her, to "give the child a name."

Such marriages often were long lived, because "divorce" was one of those words that bore the stigma of evil. Rarely was divorce even considered in Osage County after the birth of a child. Hale and Essie were married for twenty-six years before they found out they could no longer stand the sight of each other.

When they returned from their honeymoon cruise in the Caribbean, Hale hung his "Hale Witcher, Lawyer" shingle beside the stairway leading up to his office above his father's drug-store. On a bright August morning, friends dropped by to shake his hand and wish him well.

Donna Jean, skirting the group surrounding him, was walking past when their eyes met.

She saw his lips form the words, "Donna Jean."

With a quick smile, she turned away. Hale excused himself and hurried after her. "Donna Jean. Please, wait."

"Congratulations, Hale," she said. "I know you'll be a fine lawyer."

"I need to talk to you."

"Not now. Another time perhaps."

"Maybe I could call you sometime."

"What would Essie think about that?"

"Essie is too busy with her own interests to think about much else."

"Oh, yes. I see her name in the paper. Yours too, of course."

"Could you come to my office one day?" Hale said. "I'd like to show you what I've done to it."

"I might." She smiled. "Goodbye, Hale."

With his eyes he followed her down the block to Caster's Department Store.

She paused, smiled back at him, and went inside.

CHAPTER 12

Jeff Reveals His Plan

Witcher's slim, Lincolnesque frame rose from the swivel chair behind his desk. In one long stride he was at his second-story window overlooking the street below. With an open palm he made a circle on the steamy pane, and peered out through the circle at the falling rain.

He turned from the window and tugged at his graying chin whiskers, contemplating the man seated in the stuffed leather chair on the other side of his desk. He never saw him before he stuck his head in the door and asked if he could come in.

All he knew about him was what Mason Bryer told him on the phone. Jeff Timberlake, a reporter from some news gathering company. Bryer said Timberlake uncovered some new information about the Susie McCord case. Witcher got interested.

He was thinking about Susie lately, pondering whether he was the only one who cared any more what happened to her. Now, this Timberlake fellow pops in with a tale about being offered money by the man whose grandson was the last one to see Susie alive.

"Mr. Timberlake," Witcher said, with an easy, meditative drawl. "Do you have any idea what you're up against here?"

"The man offered me money," Jeff said. "You'll have to tell me what the legal implications are."

"For the sake of what if," Witcher said, "what if it really was a bribery attempt by a man whose grandson has been suspect from the beginning? What do we do with it? You were there, Amos was there, and the black man was there. But we don't know who heard what, do we?"

"I know what I heard," Jeff said. "He said how much would it take?"

"Well, now I'm not questioning what you heard, but it would help a lot if we knew Waldo heard it too. Amos is not about to admit it, so if Waldo didn't hear what you say Amos said, all we've got to go on is your word against Amos's. And that's about as conclusive as a pig squealing contest at the county fair.

"This thing has been lying dormant for four years. Blake Baldwin was the county attorney at the time, and he ruled it accidental drowning—with the help of that semi-deputy they've got over there. Petty, is it?"

"Chink Petty, yes."

"Petty wouldn't recognize a murder if he

stumbled over it if there was a Marlow involved. Amos has paid his wages since day one."

"Mason Bryer thinks Baldwin was on the Marlow payroll."

"I wouldn't put it past Amos to line up as many folks as he thought it would take to cover his ass. Bryer may be right. Blake was a good prosecutor, and I guess he's a pretty good Congressman. I didn't agree at the time that Susie's death was accidental. But, Baldwin was the boss, so I didn't push it.

"That's how I got this job—after Baldwin went to Washington. Politics is a peculiar business, Mr. Timberlake. Once you get in the game, your whole life changes. Sitting on the bench, watching from the sidelines is not real exciting, so you itch to get back in there.

"The day you get elected, you get to thinking maybe you're smarter than the people who voted for you. That's the day you start working on staying in the game. Getting re-elected. That's what you live for. It's all about power. Staying in the game becomes a matter of survival.

"You soon find out there's room for only so many hogs at the trough. You start taking a little money here, and little more there, and everybody who makes a contribution wants a piece of you. You make promises, some of which you aim to keep. But there's not enough power and privilege to go around. One day you discover all the pieces of you are gone, and you're the only one who doesn't own any of them.

"You don't know who you are any more. One

morning you wake up, look in the mirror, and wonder who the hell that stranger is you're shaving."

Bryer indicated that Witcher was not "a Marlow man." Jeff wondered whose man he was. Could he be describing his own career?

"Baldwin was a good man," Witcher went on, "but politics does strange things to the players. It didn't occur to me at the time that Baldwin might call Susie's death an accident because Amos was in the picture. Now, I wouldn't be surprised if Amos had Blake in his hip pocket.

"It occurs to me that Amos is trying to buy you off too. If we can prove that, we've got ourselves a new kettle of fish with a whole different smell."

"How do we go about that?" Jeff asked.

"If we could get Waldo to say he heard Amos make the offer," Witcher said, "we'd have reason to start poking around again. That's the last thing Amos wants. Without Waldo's corroboration, though, we don't have much to go on." He cocked his head to one side. "How did you know Susie?"

"I didn't know her," Jeff answered. "I came to Marlow on another matter and saw that sign on the high-way. I was curious to know the story behind it. A friend of mine at NNS in Des Moines put me on assignment to find out."

"And—?"

"About the only thing I've learned for sure is that the dead girl's mother paid for the billboard advertising her death."

"Her mother?"

"That's what Harvey Wilcox said."

"Did Wilcox put up the sign?"

"Yes. He said the money Hilda left to pay for it runs out this month. I would guess Hilda didn't think Susie's death was an accident, and spent the money for the sign to get back at the town for killing her daughter."

Witcher's face split into a broad smile.

"Amos laid a bucketful of greenbacks in Hilda's lap after Susie's funeral," he said. "That means the billboard was paid for with Amos's money."

"That doesn't make Randy look any better, does it?" Jeff said.

"Every time Amos makes a move, the boy looks more guilty," Witcher said. "Amos is scared stiff of what might be uncovered if people were free to talk about it."

Jeff's ears perked up. "Do they still have town hall meetings around here?"

"Not often, but if it's important enough. Why?"

"What if we had an open meeting where people could say anything they want about what happened to Susie?"

Witcher fingered his chin whiskers. "That might work. What have you got in mind?"

Jeff wanted to tell Witcher about Hack and Jason, but still thought he should talk to the boys first. Even so, if there was to be a public meeting, the county attorney needed to know what Amy told him. "There's something else you need to know."

"Yeah?"

"Just this afternoon, I learned there are witnesses who put Randy Marlow on the bridge when Susie was last seen alive."

"Witnesses?"

"Yes, sir. A couple of boys camping out near the bridge that night."

"You mean eyewitnesses?" Witcher was aghast. "Somebody who actually saw what took place out there?"

"That's what they told one of their teachers this morning."

"A couple of boys, you say. Who are they? Big boys, little boys? What kind of boys are we talking about here?"

"Teenagers."

"Well, where the hell are they? This is the first solid development we've had in four years. Where have they been all this time?"

"Like everybody else, they've been afraid to talk about it—till now. Would you like me to bring them in for an interview?"

"Hell yes!" Witcher scratched his head. "No, wait. Are you serious about that town meeting?"

"Only if you will be in charge. I don't know much about legal procedure."

"When?"

"Tomorrow afternoon."

The idea was less than a minute old, and Jeff hoped he could put it together that fast. If he could get Mason to print some posters overnight, that would give him a leg up. He'd have to depend on Amy to arrange with the school for the gym as a meeting place.

"Tomorrow afternoon," Witcher said. "That doesn't give us much time."

"I don't have much time. Petty is itching to ride

me out of town on a rail if I'm not gone by sundown tomorrow."

Witcher flipped through his desk calendar. "I've got to be in Kansas City tomorrow night," he said. "If we can set this thing up for around two o'clock, that'll give me time to make it."

Jeff was on his feet. "Can I call you tonight if I don't get it done?"

Witcher rummaged through a desk drawer and came up with a white business card, scribbled something on the back, and handed it to Jeff. "I put my home number on the back. If I don't answer, one of those recording contraptions will. Just tell me when and where"

On his way out, Jeff said, "If you don't hear from me, I'll see you at the Marlow High School gym tomorrow at two."

Witcher watched him go, fondled his chin whiskers, and gave his head a thoughtful shake. "His mother must have been part whirlwind," he mused.

Again he peered through the circle on the window. He saw Donna Jean dodging puddles, crossing the street to her car. A white umbrella protected her head from the rain. She got into her black Buick parked in front of the Post Office and drove away.

Witcher would bet his bird egg blue 1956 Continental that Donna Jean smiled when she looked up at his window. He didn't smile.

His phone rang. He picked it up. "Yes, Mr. Marlow. He just left. Yes, sir." Witcher dropped the phone in its cradle. He caught sight of his Missouri

Bar Association certificate framed on the wall. He studied it for a long moment, recalling the years of strenuous effort and sleepless nights he invested in qualifying for the document. More important was his sworn commitment to abide by the Rules of Professional Conduct, and to the law, in pursuit of justice.

Witcher shook his head. "No, Mr. Marlow," he said.

Jeff Picks up a Hiker

Jeff put up an arm to shield his face from the rain and made a dash for the Corvette. He switched on the ignition, heard the motor kick in, spun out of the parking space, and headed west toward Marlow. Seven minutes later he saw someone walking along the road. Whoever it was would appreciate a chance to get out of the rain. He pulled alongside and braked to a stop. It was Jackie Marlow. He threw the passenger side door open. "Jackie!" he said. "Get in."

She hopped in, soaking wet. "I blew a tire and wound up in a ditch."

"What about the spare?"

"No spare. I never had it fixed from last time."

"There must be a gas station along here where we can get help," Jeff said. "There's a box of Kleenex on the back seat."

Jackie reached for the Kleenex and wiped her rain wet face.

Jeff shifted into gear. "Where were you going?"

"To the University to see Randy. After you and I

talked this morning, I decided it was time I got some things straight with my father. It was not a pleasant experience." She shook her tousled, rain-soaked head. "I feel so sorry for him. He has given up on Randy. He's scared to death Randy killed Susie, and it's eating him alive."

Jeff couldn't tell whether her eyes were wet from rain, or for the sadness she felt for her father.

"I've got to be with my son," she said. "One way or the other, I need him to tell me the truth."

"You know I met with your father too."

"Yes, he told me about that. You've stirred up a hornet's nest, and he doesn't know how to handle it. Actually, I'm not sure myself any more. Why do I have the feeling you want my son to be guilty?"

"I don't want anybody to be guilty, but somebody is. What I want is to get at the truth."

"Whatever that is," she said. "I read some place truth is not always what it appears to be.

"Looking innocent is as important as being innocent. That's part of my father's problem. He doesn't want to face the truth because of what it might look like."

Jeff spotted a gas station, and pulled under the canopy.

"Are you sure you'll be okay?" he said, braking to a stop.

"I'll be fine." A smile brightened her rain-streaked face. "I see they've got a tow truck. I'll be out of here in no time."

"Can you have Randy in Marlow tomorrow at two o'clock?"

"Tomorrow? Why?"

"I just came from a meeting with Hale Witcher, the county attorney."

He wasn't ready to tell her why he went to see Witcher, that her father offered him money to forget about Susie. Nor was he going to mention Amy's news about the boys seeing Randy at the bridge the night Susie died. Jackie already had enough on her mind to keep her grieving apparatus churning for a while. Whatever else she needed to know she could find out at the meeting tomorrow. He wanted to be sure she brought Randy to hear what was said, to confirm or deny.

"Witcher agreed to be at a town meeting where people can say what they want about Susie's death," Jeff said. "Randy needs to be there."

She cast him a sharp look. "Are they going to crucify my son?"

"There will be no crucifixion. The town has been bottled up for four years. If they have a chance to blow off some steam, maybe in the process something good will come of it. Your guess is as good as mine what it might be. Witcher doesn't believe it was accidental drowning. He's thinking foul play. Somebody's guilty. We need to find out who it is."

"Okay. Where and when?"

"I've got to work out the details, and I don't have much time. The marshal gave me till sundown tomorrow to wind up my business and clear out of Dodge."

"That's my father's doing. What is your business?"

"A man named Zachary Wheeler. I haven't

found anybody who ever knew him. Wheeler was a friend of my mother's. She died recently and asked me to look him up."

"I'm sorry about your mother. So, you haven't found Wheeler?"

"No. Susie got in the way."

"Did you ask my father about him?"

"Your father and I had other things to talk about," he said. "No, I didn't ask him."

"Okay." She pushed the car door open. "So, what about tomorrow?"

"Two o'clock at the high school."

"Can I do something to help?"

"Be sure Randy shows up."

"I can do that," Jackie said.

"What about your father? He needs to be there too."

"I don't know. You never can tell what he's going to do any more."

"Bring him with you, Jackie. You know there's a lot of resentment in town toward the Marlow family because of Susie."

"I know. It hasn't always been that way. Things began to change when my mother was killed in that car wreck. After Susie died, it got worse." She stepped out of the car.

"Two o'clock tomorrow?"

"We'll be there."

He watched her safely inside, then moved the Corvette onto the blacktop, and stepped on the gas. The rain brought early darkness, and Jeff flipped on the headlights. Near the Marlow city limits he waited for a light to change. In the rearview mirror he saw a man get out of a black pickup close behind him. A three-count later his passenger side door flew open and the man slid in beside him, slammed the door shut, and waved a handgun.

"What the hell are you doing?" Jeff asked.

"Just drive, man, and don't gimme no shit."

Jeff started to resist. The young hoodlum nudged his jaw with the pistol.

"Straight west till I tell you to stop," the kid said in a high-pitched voice.

Jeff drove. His contacts with police taught him the best way to deal with a loony like this one was to keep calm. If he showed any sign of fear or panic, the man with the gun would react the same way, and Jeff could wind up dead. He pegged the gunman at about twenty years old.

Even in the semi-darkness, Jeff's eyes were drawn to the perfectly formed, pearly white teeth. The punk's slick shaved face was pale as a baby's bottom, and a shock of wavy blond hair swept his shoulders. *Keep it light*, Jeff told himself. Don't do anything that might set him off. "Is that a real gun?"

The gunman was in no mood for jokes. "Shut up and drive, man."

"You're not going to shoot me, are you?"

"I'm thinking about it."

"Why don't you do it now and get it over with?"

"Just drive the damn car, man!"

Jeff's mind was busy working on a plan of action. "Who does your hair?"

"What?"

"Your hair, man. Who does it?"

A pleased grin appeared on the young hoodlum's

face. "I do," he said.

"Nice."

"They don't call me Pretty Boy for nothin'."

"Pretty Boy?" Jeff thought he had found a weak spot. "Is that your real name?"

"My mama calls me—" He stopped short, and poked the gun under Jeff's jaw. "Knock off the shit and drive, man!"

Jeff felt the gun waver unsteadily against his jaw. Pretty Boy was more nervous than he. He knew he'd better make his move before Pretty Boy panicked and blew his head off. "How far?"

"I'll tell you when to stop. There's a cozy little spot where I'm gonna do you."

"You better do it now, Pretty Boy. No telling what might happen before we get there."

"Knock off the shit."

"Okay, Pretty Boy, hang on!" Jeff leaned on the accelerator and the Corvette shot forward like Sea Biscuit out of the gate. The needle nudged seventy, seven-five, eighty. Pretty Boy's lips curled into a nervous twist, and Jeff knew he had him.

"Hey, man," Pretty Boy said. "You better slow this sucker down!"

Jeff kept driving, dodging on-coming cars, careening past others on the rain-slick blacktop.

"Slow down or I'll blow your head off!" Pretty Boy screamed.

"Go ahead. If I go, you go."

"Pull over! Stop the goddam car. Now!"

Pretty Boy was frantic. Jeff knew the right moment had come. "Okay, Pretty Boy, here's what you're going to do. Toss the gun in the back, and stand on your head on the floor."

"No, man," Pretty Boy whimpered, "I ain't gonna—"

"Do it, dammit, or I'll kill us both!" Jeff yelled. "On your head or your mama will pick you up with a blotter!" Pretty Boy threw the door open, and rolled out of the car into the ditch. The door banged shut, and Jeff gunned it out of there. He never looked back. A mile down the road he screeched the Corvette to a stop and slumped against the wheel. Chink Petty would know where to find the punk called Pretty Boy.

Jeff Unloads

Jeff snapped up Amy's phone, dialed the number she gave him, and listened for the ring. He hoped Petty was still in his office. Chink answered and listened while Jeff described the Pretty Boy incident. "Is this how things go down in Marlow?" Jeff shouted into the phone.

Chink knew he was furious. "I don't work that way."

"Well, somebody works that way, and I think we both know who it is."

"I'll look into it."

"You do that, Mr. Petty. And be sure to let Mr. Marlow know who filed the complaint."

Jeff slammed the phone down, and ran a hand across his face, red with anger.

To Amy, he said, "He said he'd look into it."

Amy rolled her eyes.

Chink's Pretty Boy Hunt

The white Fairlane crawled along the narrow street, sloshing through deep-rutted mud.

Chink squinted into the darkness, looking from one side of the street to the other. He could use the spotlights, but he didn't want to disturb the neighborhood. All he wanted was to locate one house and a blond-haired punk called Pretty Boy. Chink knew who he was—a petty thief and purse snatcher. He'd hauled Pretty Boy in for such offenses and fed him on county money before. But this caper against Timberlake was a major maneuver for the small time hood.

Petty heard rumors of a move against the man in the red Corvette, but put little stock in them. He didn't expect the strong armed action that Timberlake described. The rain made it difficult, but Chink would recognize the house when he saw it.

He took a moment to focus on the small frame house with paint peeling off its sides. He parked at the curb and ambled up to the door, wishing he'd slipped on his rain jacket against the cold drizzle. He gave the door a solid rap, got no answer. He knocked again. Still no answer. He opened the screen and pounded on the wooden door. "Pretty Boy!"

Chink tried to convince himself Amos had nothing to do with Pretty Boy's caper. Even paranoid as Amos was, he doubted the man would resort to such drastic measures to prevent some stranger from asking questions about a dead girl. He rationalized it was more likely a screwball attempt by Pretty Boy to high-jack the red Corvette. Still, he questioned whether Pretty Boy was smart enough to plan such a trick on his own.

The jeering image of Buck Farrell crossed his mind. Farrell was the leader of a gang of black leather jackets on the edge of the law. Chink knew where to find Farrell, and as soon as he settled with Pretty Boy, Buck would be his next stop.

"Open up this door and come on out here, Pretty Boy," Chink yelled at the door. "I know you're in there."

Chink didn't know Pretty Boy was in there. He hoped he was in there. He worked himself into a sweat because the plug ugly pulled such a stupid stunt in his town. He was in the mood to rack somebody's ass, and Pretty Boy gave him a reason to get it done.

"I'm giving you a ten-count to show your ugly face, Pretty Boy, or I'm coming in after you," Chink said, "and I'm already up to five."

Slowly the door creaked open. Chink fired his flashlight on Pretty Boy's bruised face. Pretty Boy's right arm was in a sling. "You been sorting wildcats again, boy?"

"No, I ain't been sortin' no wildcats."

"How'd you get all beat up like that?"

"My girlfriend scratched me up some."

"Uh-huh." Chink grabbed him by the chin and jerked it from side to side. "She did one hell of a job on you, boy. I thought maybe you got that way jumping out of a car going ninety miles an hour." Pretty Boy squirmed. "What I hear," Chink said, "you've got some friends who don't like cleaning up the shit from the dumb stuff you do. After this, I bet they'll work you over so you'll wish you never saw a red Corvette." He gave Pretty Boy time to think about that. "I wouldn't be surprised if one of them reported you dead by morning."

Pretty Boy shifted uneasily from one foot to the other.

"Are you scared, boy?" Chink said.

Pretty Boy blinked, but said nothing. Without the gun he was just another punk kid.

"You sure as hell better be scared. I'm gonna have a chat with Buck about this. I have an idea he'll put that other arm in a sling."

"Buck who?"

Chink came within a one count of smacking him across the mouth. "You know damn well Buck who. The slimy bastard that put you up to that caper a while ago."

"Didn't nobody put me up to nothin'."

Chink's eyes narrowed to suspicious slits.

"Are you telling me you cooked that one up all by yourself?"

"I don't know nothin' about no damn red Corvette."

"Uh-huh. When Buck gets through with you, you'll wish you never knew nothin' about him either. He won't get his jollies out of me coming down on him for one of your stupid ass tricks."

Pretty Boy squirmed.

"Is your daddy home?" Chink said.

"Ain't got no daddy."

Chink grunted, and aimed the flashlight dead in

Pretty Boy's eyes. "From the looks of you, I'd say you never had no mama either."

Pretty Boy rousted up enough courage to say, "You won't be so damn cocky when the man finds out about this."

"What man is that, Pretty Boy?"

"You know what man. He'll skin your ass and nail it to the City Hall door."

Chink resisted the temptation to grind Pretty Boy under the sharp heel of his cowboy boot, the same as any other insect. "You scare the hell out of me, boy." He didn't push it. He wasn't sure he wanted to hear the name Pretty Boy might blurt out. He cuffed him gently under the chin with a folded fist. "You be a good boy now, you hear? I'll tell old Buck you said howdy."

The Search for Hack Peebles

The Santa Fe freight train broadcast its mournful warning of its passing though Old Town.

The rumble of boxcars, creaking under the weight of wonders bound for someplace else, was commonplace as the potholes in Old Town's muddy streets.

Jeff, with Amy at his side, steered the Corvette across the Bois D'Arc River bridge into a world of narrow streets, dim lights, and smaller houses than those on the other side of the river. The tantalizing aroma of smoking beef and pork wafted from hickory-fired barbecue pits.

Young people, black and white, defied the rain for the fun of romping in the glow of the streetlights. Some paused to look, but most ignored the red car sloshing along past the water tower, the pool hall, the mom-and-pop grocery store, and the rows of weather-beaten clapboard houses for which Amos's mill hands paid him twelve dollars a week.

The train rumbled away, and the echo of its clickity-clack on the rails faded in the distance.

Jeff squinted between swipes of the windshield wipers. "Are you sure this is where Hack said he'd be?"

She pointed to a gas station on the right. "Maybe they could tell us something."

Jeff pulled under the canopy. He stopped beside two scarred green gas pumps. The only light was from a dim yellow bulb dangling from a cord in the front window. They waited for some sign of life. There was none. Jeff poked his head in the door. Amy followed him inside. The sound of muffled voices sifted from a back room.

Jeff eased open the door. Six pairs of black eyes pinned him where he stood. A single bare bulb hung over a table draped with a dingy brown blanket. In the middle of the blanket was a swirl of greenbacks and a pair of dice. Six black men stood around the table. All eyes focused on Jeff.

The right hand of the big man nearest the door was wrapped in a red bandanna. Covering brass knuckles, Jeff guessed. The man stared at Jeff. His arms were like tree trunks, his face a road map of knife scars.

"This is a private party, man," the man said, his voice a rumble. His thick lips curled into a challenging dare, revealing scraggly, tobacco stained teeth. "I don't 'member invitin' you."

Jeff spread his palms in a gesture of calm. "I'm not looking for trouble."

"What are you lookin' for, man?"

"Hack Peebles."

The five other men made a menacing move toward Jeff. The big man put out a hand and they stopped. Their eyes shot darts at the intruder.

Jeff said, "I thought you might tell us where to find him."

"Us?"

Jeff stood aside, and Amy stepped into the doorway.

"Miz Amy," the rumbler rumbled, surprised.

"High-bo," she said.

High-bo moved his head toward Jeff. "He with you?"

"Yes," she said. "Jeff Timberlake."

"The red Corvette guy." To Jeff, High-bo said, "Lookin' for Hack, huh?"

"Yes."

"Why you lookin' for 'im?"

"Hack was a friend of Susie McCord. He knows something about how she died. I want to talk to him about that."

The six checked each other with silent stares.

"Susie," High-bo said. "You some kind o' cop, or what?"

"No, no cop."

"Hack ain't here. He don't come here much no more, especially on Friday." High-bo picked up the dice and rattled them in his left hand. "Hack go to church on Friday."

Jeff looked at Amy, and she nodded. She knew the church. High-bo had a reputation for blowing his cool without provocation. Amy wanted to get out of there before he got hostile. Jeff followed her out.

"You never seen nothin' here!" High-bo threatened to their backs.

"No way," Jeff said.

Jeff and Amy didn't take an easy breath until they were safely in the car. Jeff started the motor and crawled out of the station in search of the church where High-bo said they would find Hack Peebles.

The air shivered with the spirited voices of a choir, drawing Jeff and Amy to a white frame building with a cross mounted on its steeple. They climbed the concrete steps to the front entrance.

A gray-haired black man greeted them with a smile and ushered them into the sanctuary. The choir rocked the foundation.

"Father, Son, and Holy Ghost, where you gonna be when I need you most?

The choir echoed the words.

"I tell you where you gonna be, walking right here by the side of me."

They found Hack Peebles. He was the lead singer, dancing, prancing, gyrating with the frenzied emotion of the music. Behind Hack the choir members clapped hands and stamped feet.

Hack pleaded, "Tell me, Lord, where are you now?"

The choir repeated, "Tell me, Lord, where are you now?"

"There ain't no trouble too big for you, so take my hand and lead me through. Father, Son, and Holy Ghost—" Hack spread his feet wide. His arms reached for the ceiling, and a wide grin lit his sweat-shiny face. He bowed low to the floor to wild applause and "amens". He stood up, and caught the eye of the gray-haired usher. The usher nodded. Hack made his way through the crowd to the back of the sanctuary.

"Miz Amy!" Hack said with a broad smile. "Are you sure you're in the right church?"

"Hello, Hack," she said. "You know Jeff Timberlake."

"The guy in the red Corvette."

"Right," Jeff said. "Miss Kraft says you saw what happened at the bridge the night Susie McCord died."

Hack looked at Amy for approval, questioning whether he should say anything.

"It's okay, Hack," she said.

"Yes, sir," Hack said. "Me and Jase did."

"We're having a meeting at the school tomorrow," Jeff said. "We'd like you to come and tell us what you saw. Will you do that?"

Again Hack sought permission from Amy. He got it.

"There'll be some other people there," she said. "All they want is for you and Jason to tell what you told me this morning. Okay, Hack?"

"If you say so, Miz Amy."

"Jason needs to be there too," Jeff said.

"I'll bring Jase."

"And, Hack," Amy said, "we'll have some

posters about the meeting we'd like you and Jason to put in the stores around town. Would you do that for us?"

"Tell me where."

"They'll be at the newspaper office. I'll tell Mr. Bryer you'll pick them up."

Hack went back to church, and Jeff and Amy left.

Jeff squeezed her hand. "We're on our way," he said.

Buck Farrell

Chink guided the cruiser into the knee high grass and weeds in the yard of an abandoned farm house. He eased it toward where Buck Farrell and a dozen of his Harley-humping cronies squatted around an open fire, popping cans of beer. From somewhere a radio blared the voice of Jerry Lee Lewis romping through "Great Balls of Fire."

Ferrell was deep-chested and sharp-eyed. His thin lips worked their way into a crooked smile as he watched Petty get out of the cruiser and amble toward the circle of motorcycles. Petty asked if anybody knew anything about the red Corvette incident. He was not surprised nobody did.

To Ferrell, Chink said, "We need to talk."

Ferrell tossed his buddies a careless smirk and followed Chink to the back of a small out building. Chink ripped out his gun and buried it in Ferrell's belly. Buck doubled over and grabbed his stomach.

Chink clutched Buck's throat, banged his head against the wall of the building, and rammed the muzzle of the pistol against his chin. Buck moaned in pain. His eyes bugged out.

"Now, let me tell you something, bad boy," Chink said. "I know your little Pretty Boy was mixed up in that red Corvette deal. I know it wasn't his idea, because he's not smart enough to find his ass without a road map. So, let me tell you one thing, and you had better get it through that thick skull of yours. If I ever so much as dream about you or one of your asshole buddies being involved in anything bigger than a Sunday School picnic, I'm coming after you. Not them, you. The rest of them can go straight to hell as far as I'm concerned, but you I'm coming after. Now, can I count on you to get back out there and explain to those gentlemen who's in charge in this town?"

Buck nodded weakly, hugging his stomach.

"You keep telling yourself it ain't you," Chink said. He put his gun away, and handed Ferrell a handkerchief. "Wipe your face," the marshal said. "You look awful."

Ferrell wiped, and Chink left.

The Night Before

Sometime in the night Jeff heard whimpering cries from Amy's bedroom. He sat up and listened. He rolled out of bed, and followed the sound of sobbing along the carpeted hallway to Amy's bedside. Her face was framed in tousled lumps of damp bond hair. Jeff touched her face. "Amy. Amy, it's Jeff. Wake up."

Jarred awake, she cried, "Oh, Jeff!"

She threw her arms around him, and he held her close. "Are you okay?"

"I thought I saw Susie in the water. I tried to save her, but every time I got close, the current swept her farther downstream. I couldn't reach her. It was awful!"

"It's all right."

He cradled her head in his arms, stroking her hair as she clung to him. "Are you coming with me to the meeting tomorrow?" he asked.

"If you want me to."

"I do."

Knock Knock

Still in jogging mode from her morning run, Amy burst through her front door. She stripped off her sweats and shoes as she went. Half way down the hall she heard running water. Jeff was in the shower. By the time she got there, no stitch remained upon her body. Into the steamy bathroom she charged, and gave the shower door a solid rap. "Knock knock."

"Who's there?"

"Lemme."

"Lemme who?"

"Lemme in or I'll scream."

The glass shower door slid sideways.

"It's open," Jeff said.

Amy gets Nosy

In the booth off the kitchen, all toweled off and decked out in her favorite Kelly green sweats, Amy poured coffee. "How long are you going to be hanging around here?"

"Well, you know Marshal Petty. He gave me until sundown today to get out of town."

"Marshal Petty." She rolled her eyes, and poured herself a cup of coffee. "That's how you big city dudes do it, huh?" She sat down on the other side of the booth. "You blow in here, rape our women, terrorize the town and blow out again. And that's the last we ever see of you."

"That's how we do it," he said, sipping at his coffee. "Do you want to come with me when it's over?"

She stared at him, said nothing.

"Do you?" he said.

She lowered her eyes.

"Alex?" he said.

Over the rim of her cup she studied his face. No secrets there. He was leaving town and was asking her to come with him.

"Alex is a nonentity," she said.

"What then?"

"I've known you for two days, and I don't even know what you do for a living."

"Does your answer depend on what I do for a living?"

She smiled and shook her head.

"Mostly," Jeff said, "I go traipsing around the country trying to find out how little dead girls died."

"Mmhmm. You can't let it go, can you?"

"Not yet. Maybe after the meeting today."

"What about that Wheeler guy?"

"I've got to do something about him."

"Yes," she said.

"Yes what?"

"I want to come with you."

"I didn't think it would be that easy."

"Easy!"

He cupped her face in his hands and kissed her on the mouth. "Be ready," he said with a wink. "The bus could leave at any time."

The Meeting

Dottie closed the door to the diner at one-thirty and walked the six blocks to the high school. She thought she'd be the first one to arrive at the town hall meeting in the high school gym.

The principal blinked wide-eyed when Amy broached the subject the day before. "Pretty late in the day to get ready for a meeting of that size," he said. Even so, Amy persuaded him of the significance of the meeting. He reluctantly agreed to open the doors of the gym on a Saturday afternoon.

Dottie was surprised to find she was not the first one to arrive. Dozens of Marlowites streamed down the hallway past the cafeteria, the lab, the principal's office, and into the gym. She found a seat in the bleachers beside Jeff and Amy. "Is this a meeting or a wake?" Dottie said of the hushed murmuring around her.

Herb Spencer was there, along with Leland

Haymes and half a dozen other merchants. Perkins Pike was seated next to Cecil Combs on the third row up from the hardwood basketball court. Two arms' lengths to Cecil's left sat Wiley Hipp by Mason Bryer. Harvey Wilcox sat on the other side next to Bryer.

Wiley and Cecil traded looks.

Cecil's pleaded, "Don't do it, Wiley."

The townsfolk came expecting to hear Amos confess that he was wrong, and apologize for penalizing the town for four years for a dastardly deed of which they knew his grandson was guilty. Sure, it was Amos's town. Most of them worked for him, and he took care of them when they couldn't care for themselves. They appreciated what Amos did for them, but they also believed Randy escaped paying for the death of Susie McCord because he was the grandson of the man who owned the town. They brought with them the hope of hearing the truth about Randy's involvement in the death of the much loved young girl, and they would finally be free of the sentence of silence they suffered because of it.

They would be disappointed. Not only would Amos not apologize, but he would protest the proceedings as an attempt to humiliate himself and his grandson.

Nobody knew how much this Timberlake fellow knew about anything, but at least he made some folks nervous. He challenged the marshal, and didn't wilt in the presence of Amos Marlow. And he was smart enough to involve the county attorney in the meeting.

Witcher agreed to preside over the hearing. They figured the County Attorney must be as eager as they to uncover the facts of how Susie died.

Hack and Jason parked in the middle of the bottom row of bleachers, facing a wooden lectern that somebody brought from the principal's office.

Witcher was shuffling some papers on it.

Amos was sitting to Witcher's left between Chink Petty and attorney Kevin Barrickman. Mayor Fox-worthy stewed next to the young barrister. Jackie and Randy sat two rows up.

Witcher knew why Barrickman was there. Only three years out of law school, Barrickman was not highly regarded by his peers as a person, but was respected as a capable defense lawyer. He was there to watchdog the proceedings for Amos Marlow.

Mayor Foxworthy, round faced, pudgy, and nervous about anything he didn't know everything about, hadn't yet figured out what was going on. The poster he saw at Herb Spencer's barber shop said, "Let's talk about Susie. Public meeting, High School gym, 2:00 today."

"Damned if I know," Herb said in answer to the mayor's bewildered query while Herb trimmed the gray fringe around the mayor's shiny pate.

"But I'm gonna be there," Herb said. "It's probably got something to do with that red Corvette we've seen around town."

With an anxious glance at Amos, the mayor mopped his sweating brow, wondering what Amos would have to say about what Witcher had to say.

Amos ignored him.

Sandwiched between Petty and Barrickman, the diminutive Amos seethed. Not pleased with what was taking place, Amos shot Jackie and Randy an uneasy glance that said so.

When Jackie told him last night about the Saturday afternoon meeting, Amos didn't like the sound of it, and he wasn't enjoying it now. This morning he dispatched Petty to investigate "this travesty." By the time Chink got around to investigating, the damage had been done. Hack and Jason had already distributed the posters around town. One of them shouted at Amos from an easel in the lobby of his very own bank.

Amos's goatee and mustache were vying for twitching rights. He kept an eye on Witcher, wondering what he was up to, and why Witcher showed up for what Amos considered a waste of time.

Jackie squeezed Randy's hand. Randy was a handsome, square-jawed, stocky young man with brown hair and green eyes. Like his grandfather, he was not comfortable with what was going on, but his mother insisted that he come. His eyes darted from Witcher to Amos to Jackie, seeking assurance that everything would be all right. Jackie offered no guarantees. The best she could do was what she was doing already— clutching his left hand with her right.

The gathering was stunned to silence by the two o'clock rendition of "Oh, What a Beautiful Morning" that shook the building. The City Hall clock struck again.

Raymond Bell, the high school principal, made a

brief welcoming statement, and introduced the mayor for "a few words."

Foxworthy clomped to the front, fiddling with his red-and-white striped tie. With a look at Amos that said, "Am I still going to have a job when this is over?" the mayor mopped his brow, and confessed he was at a loss to explain why this meeting was taking place. He muttered back to his seat, and the crowd applauded. It wasn't clear whether their applause was in appreciation of the mayor's comments, or joyful that he shut up.

"Well, Mr. Mayor," Witcher said, "and ladies and gentlemen of Marlow, as you know, for four years there has been some mystery surrounding the death of a young lady named Susie McCord. And that, sir," he said to the befuddled mayor, "is why we're here—to give anyone who cares to do so an opportunity to talk about Susie. I was the assistant county attorney when Susie died, and was not satisfied with the determination made, nor did I believe the case should have been closed at that time. Now, as county attorney, recent developments give us cause to pursue the case, to find out whether Susie's death was an accident, as concluded by the county attorney, or something more serious."

To the mayor, he said, "Does that answer your question, sir?"

Foxworthy harrumphed and opened his mouth, but by the time he found his voice Witcher had moved on. The mayor crawled back into his shell.

"This meeting was arranged by a man named Jeff Timberlake," Witcher said. "Mr. Timberlake is here covering the Susie story for National News

Service."

Somebody said, "The red Corvette guy."

Jeff held up a hand, and the crowd applauded.

"He was in town on another matter," Witcher went on, "saw the Susie sign, and decided to find out why it was there. In the process, Mr. Timberlake uncovered some new information, which he brought to my attention, and asked me to preside here today. I have here," Witcher said, holding up a sheet of paper, "a list of people who we hope can shed some light on the matter that we are here to discuss."

Amos's eyes narrowed, wanting this thing to be over. He brushed his goatee with a nervous hand.

"As the city's leading citizen, sir," Witcher said to Amos, "and a relative of one of the major players in this drama, we'd like to hear what you have to say, if you'd care to make a statement."

Amos jabbed an elbow in Barrickman's ribs. Barrickman bounced to his feet. He was dressed in a gray double-breasted pinstripe suit, white cotton shirt, flashing diamond French cuffs, and a red silk tie. "If it's permissible, counselor," he said, "I can answer for Mr. Marlow."

"Well, it is not permissible, counselor. I addressed Mr. Marlow, and I'd like the response to come from Mr. Marlow."

Barrickman whispered something to Amos. Amos glared at Witcher, got to his feet, and limped forward a couple of steps.

"Only this, Mr. Witcher," Amos said, his voice tinged with anger. "If something useful comes out of this meeting, I will cooperate to the fullest. If not, I will expect an apology to the good people of the city of Marlow."

Witcher gave his head a solemn nod, the significance of which only he and Amos understood: Witcher was there to discover facts, and let the chips fall where they may.

"You shall have your apology, sir, if it comes to that," Witcher said. "And now, ladies and gentlemen, let me remind you this is not a court of law, but a public forum. Anyone who doesn't care to participate is under no obligation to do so. You are free to go at any time. If you choose to stay, you are encouraged to speak your mind without restraint."

Nobody left.

Witcher consulted his list. "Is Randy Marlow here?" he asked.

Amos sought out his grandson, and found him sitting next to Jackie with a sullen look on his face. He glared at Witcher.

All eyes went to the upper tier, seeking the person of Randy Marlow. Jackie nudged Randy, and he raised his hand.

Amos squirmed in his seat, and shot a dart at Chink that said, "Why don't you get off your skinny ass and do something about this?"

Chink scratched his nose and looked the other way.

"Randy," Witcher said, "it has been established that you were the last person to see Susie McCord alive. We have two young men who will testify they saw you and Susie together on the Bois D'Arc River bridge the night she died."

I-told-you-so nods, and satisfied smiles circled

the gathering.

Randy stirred uneasily.

Jackie leaned forward with a worried look on her face. Why didn't Timberlake tell me about the witnesses yesterday?

She tried to catch his eye, but Jeff was watching Amos.

Amos limped to his feet and shook a fist at Witcher. Barrickman restrained him with a hand on his arm. Amos sat down, and stared at Randy.

Randy sought support with a pleading look at his mother. Jackie clutched his hand so hard her knuckles turned white.

To Randy, Witcher said, "Before we hear from you, however, I'm going to ask the boys, Hack and Jason, to tell us what they saw at the bridge the night of Sept. 18, 1954."

What Happened, Guys?

Jason and Hack drifted off to sleep beside their campfire on the bank of the Bois D'Arc River. Swollen by recent rains, the river flooded their usual camping spot, forcing them to move to higher ground.

Sometime in the night the boys were jarred awake by the screech of tires on the gravel road leading across the bridge to Old Town.

"What's that?" Jason said.

"Up on the road," Hack said.

"Get away from me!" they heard a girl's voice yell.

The boys scrambled to their feet and bounded up

the grassy slope. A half dozen barefoot leaps brought them to the edge of the road where they flattened out on their stomachs.

In bright moonlight they saw a Chevrolet convertible with the top down parked near the bridge. In the front seat, a boy was grabbing at a girl. The girl was fighting him off.

"No! Leave me alone!" she shouted.

"Aw, come on!"

"Stop it, Randy! Stay away from me!"

Randy? The boys looked at each other, wide-eyed.

The girl bolted from the car, and ran toward the bridge. It was Susie McCord. She lived in Old Town. Jason and Hack sometimes walked with her to school.

"You're not walking home!" Randy yelled. He leaped out of the car and ran after her. "I said I'd take you home," Randy yelled, "and that's sure as hell what I'm gonna do!"

It was Randy all right. Jackie's bastard kid and Amos's grandson.

The boys heard scuffling feet on the bridge's wooden deck. They heard Randy say, "Come on, Susie, get back in the car. Ouch! Damn you, Susie!"

Susie screamed. The boys heard a loud splash in the water. Randy called to her, but she didn't answer. A minute later Hack and Jason ducked out of sight.

Randy came stumbling along the river bank. "Susie!" Randy called. He kept running and calling, "Susie, Susie!"

There was no answer.

Randy ran back to his car, frantically whimpering and breathing hard, as if afraid something terrible happened. He got in his car, spun it around, splattering gravel, headed toward town at high speed.

Jason leaped to his feet. Hack caught his arm. "We gotta do something, Hack."

"It's too late, man.," Hack said. "Randy couldn't find her. We can't find her either."

"Come on, Hack, we can't just let her—"

"Ain't nothing we can do, Jase. Susie's gone."

Jason wiped his eyes. "We gotta tell somebody," he cried.

"Who we gonna tell—his mama? His grand daddy? That's Randy Marlow we're talking about, Jase. If we tell 'em what we saw, next thing they'd be doing is throwing us in jail like we done it."

Jason hung his head.

Hack placed an arm across his friend's trembling shoulders. "Let's go home, Jase."

The gathering flashed smug smiles as the boys finished their story. Getting even with Amos, confirming what they knew from the beginning— Randy Marlow killed Susie McCord.

Randy's face was a muddle of confusion.

Jackie's eyes were locked on Hack and Jason, trying to convince herself that what they said they saw, they did not see.

Mason Bryer scribbled feverishly in his notepad.

Amos glared at Barrickman.

The lawyer tried to object, but Witcher ignored him.

The mayor ventured a question. "How do we

know the girl on the bridge was Susie McCord?"

The boys identified her, but it was beyond the mayor's attention span.

Witcher reminded him his question was answered, but asked the boys any way.

"How do we know the girl on the bridge was Susie McCord?"

"Randy called her Susie," Hack said.

"Circumstantial!" Barrickman protested. He jumped to his feet, waving an arm at Witcher. "Unfounded!" he shouted.

"We knew Susie," Jason said. "We saw her run from the car."

A woman in the upper tier said, "Whose body did they drag out of the river?"

"Susie McCord's," rose a chorus of voices. "Where have you been for the last four years?"

"Cecil Combs," Witcher said. "Is Mr. Combs here?"

Cecil was there, but he wasn't anxious to participate in the proceedings.

All eyes saw him raise a limp hand.

"Mr. Combs," Witcher said, "whose body did you carry from the Bois D'Arc River on Sunday morning, September 19, 1954?"

"Susie McCord's," Cecil mumbled.

"Louder," somebody shouted. "We can't hear you."

Cecil said it again, louder.

"Are we agreed then," Witcher said, "the girl Randy Marlow took to the party, drove to the bridge, scuffled with, and chased after along the river, was the same girl whose body was recovered from the Bois D'Arc River on Sunday morning, September 19, 1954?"

"Objection!" It was Barrickman again, playing lawyer at Amos's urging.

"It has not been established that the girl Randy Marlow took to the party was the same girl witnesses allege they saw with him at the bridge."

"Bear with us, Mr. Barrickman," Witcher said. "Is there anyone here who can verify Susie McCord was the girl Randy Marlow took to the party that Saturday night?"

Amy looked at Jeff. He nodded, and she raised her hand.

Witcher checked his list.

"Are you Miss Kraft?"

"Yes."

"And what can you tell us?"

"I saw Randy pick Susie up that night before the party."

"How did you know it was Susie?"

"I teach PE here at the high school, and do Park and Rec for the city in the summer. Susie used to help out with the younger kids."

"How did she help out?"

"She was good at softball, volley ball, soccer. Whatever she did, she did well. The only thing she didn't help with was swimming."

"Why was that?"

"Susie couldn't swim. She was afraid of water."

"Do you know why she was afraid of water?"

"I know why." It was Dottie. She stood up, and said, "I'm Dottie. Susie worked for me at the diner after school and weekends. She told me once when she was little she almost drowned in a pool. She wouldn't even take a bath in a tub. She always took a shower."

"In view of this testimony," Witcher said, "is it reasonable to conclude that Susie did not willingly get into the Bois D'Arc River?"

"Damn right!" Dottie said to chuckles all around.

Witcher said, "Miss Kraft, how do you know Randy Marlow?"

"Everybody knows Randy. He's Jackie's kid, and Mr. Marlow's grandson."

Amos hid behind a trembling hand, and Jackie hugged her son.

"You've told us," Witcher said, "you saw Randy pick Susie up. Will you explain how that came about?"

"I was stopped at the light near Dottie's Diner at closing time. I saw Susie come out of the diner and lock the door. A car was parked across the street. I heard someone in the car call Susie's name. She walked across the street and got in the car, and it pulled away. The light changed, and I turned left onto Mulberry. I saw Randy at the wheel of the car."

"And you can positively identify Randy Marlow as the driver of that car?"

"Yes, sir. He was as close to me as you are. He even waved to me."

"Can you describe the car?"

"It was one of those smaller ones. I don't know what kind, but it was a convertible with the top down."

"So you got a good look at both people in the

car?"

"Yes, sir."

"There is no doubt in your mind, four years later, that it was Susie McCord who got in the car with Randy Marlow?"

"No, sir."

"Can you tell us whether they went from there to the party?"

"I don't know."

"Thank you, Miss Kraft." To the audience, Witcher said, "Is there anyone here who can verify that Randy and Susie arrived at the party together?"

"I can."

Four rows up in the bleachers a young, dark haired woman stood up and identified herself as Kathy Thomas. "I was at the party when Randy and Susie came in," Kathy said.

"You saw them arrive together?" Witcher asked.

"I did."

"And you saw them together during the party?"

"Well, you know, off and on."

"And did you see them leave the party together?"

"No, I did not."

Witcher thanked Miss Thomas. He turned to Hack and Jason. "Boys," he said, "before we let you go, will you tell us why you waited so long to come forward with what you told us here today?"

Jason and Hack looked at each other, wondering who should go first, neither wanting to. The crowd waited.

"Well," Hack said, "it being Randy and all, we were scared if we told anybody about Susie they'd put it off on us, like we done it."

"And why have you come forward now? Are you no longer scared?"

"The guy in the red Corvette," Jason said. "He and Miz Amy—we thought they'd believe what we said."

"We thought he wouldn't be afraid to do something," Hack said, "'cause he don't live here."

All eyes focused on the stewing Amos.

Witcher dismissed the boys, and they went back to their seats.

Witcher said to Randy, "Why don't you come down here, and tell us what you remember about what happened that night?"

Randy didn't want to tell them anything. He came to the meeting only because his mother dragged him away from school. He was in a surly mood. Jackie jabbed an elbow in his ribs, and Randy stood up. He traded anxious looks with his grandfather, as though expecting him to call an immediate halt to the proceedings and send everybody home. Randy climbed down the bleachers and took a seat in the chair beside the lectern.

"Now, Randy," Witcher said, "you've heard these folks testify that you picked up Susie at Dottie's Diner the night she died. They say you scuffled with her at the bridge after she left your car. And we've established it was Susie's body recovered from the river the next morning. Is there any question in your mind that their accounts of these events are accurate?"

"I don't remember everything," Randy said. "That was a long time ago."

"Why don't you just tell us what you do remember about Saturday night, September 18, 1954?"

"I remember taking Susie to the party. We hung out there for a while. I had a few beers. Susie said she wanted to go home. I said I'd take her. When we got to the bridge—she—she got mad at me for—She started yelling at me. She got out of the car and ran to the bridge .I remember running after her, but I don't remember what happened after that."

"Do you mean you never remembered, or that you cannot now recall what happened after that?"

"I don't remember."

"You say you had a few beers. Did Susie have a few beers too?"

"No. Susie never drank. She hated it."

"Is it possible, because you had a few beers, maybe you were too drunk to realize what you were doing?"

"Objection!" Barrickman protested. "It has not been established that Mr. Marlow had too much to drink."

Witcher tried to ignore Barrickman, but it wasn't easy. He took a deep breath, and said to Randy, "You've heard the boys testify that at the bridge you and Susie were screaming at each other. Do you agree with that?"

"I don't remember."

"I'll ask you again. Because of the few beers you say you had, could you have struck Miss McCord, breaking her neck, without knowing you did it?"

"Objection! Intimidating and badgering,"

Barrickman said.

"Your objection is noted, counselor," Witcher said, on the edge of his patience. "Need I remind you that this is a public forum, and I can ask Mr. Marlow whatever I wish? If you want to examine him, you'll have your turn."

Amos popped up off his bench and limped toward Witcher, shaking a fist. "My grandson is not on trial here, sir. I'll thank you to remember that!"

"I appreciate your concern, Mr. Marlow. However, your grandson is one of the two people involved in this tragedy, and the other one is dead. Whatever he knows, we have a right to hear."

Witcher did a strange thing. Striding to where Amos's ire reached the boiling point, Witcher placed an arm across Amos's narrow shoulders. "Don't push it, Amos," Witcher whispered.

He fought the temptation to hit the little old man with a charge of attempted bribery, but abandoned it for the moment. There would be time for that later if he decided to pursue it.

Amos's dark eyes flashed with anger.

Witcher returned to the lectern. In a voice loud enough for all to hear, he said, "Mr. Marlow, I must inform you this whole town may be on trial here."

The crowd stirred uneasily. Jeff and Amy leaned forward to catch every word.

"If it develops that Miss McCord died as a result of foul play," Witcher went on, "and if it is discovered the people of Marlow were aware of it, and nobody came forward with the information, it could constitute conspiracy to impede the due process of law."

A stunned hush fell over the gathering. Questioning frowns and apprehensive squirming evinced their discomfort.

"Why, that old son-of-a-bitch!" Witcher heard a man's loud whisper.

"Even so, our purpose," Witcher said, "is not to point fingers, but to get at the truth. Now then," he said to Randy, "I need to ask you one question that might bring this forum to a close."

Randy met his mother's anxious gaze. Jackie covered her mouth with a mangled Kleenex.

Amos stiffened. He didn't want to hear the question, much less the answer.

The crowd eagerly awaited Randy's response. They lived with the answer for four years.

"The events described here," Witcher said, "indicate that you, Randy Marlow, were the last person to see Susie McCord alive. And so, on the basis of that discovery, I ask you, did you, Randy Marlow, break Susie McCord's neck in that scuffle, causing her death? And did you—"

Jackie screamed, "No!"

Amos scrambled forward in a fury, but Chink and Barrickman each caught an arm and held him back.

Randy shook his head. "No!"

"—and did you throw her body in the Bois D'Arc River, causing her to be swept downstream and against those jagged rocks?"

"No! I didn't kill her"

"Well, Randy," Witcher said, "if you can't remember anything after you chased her to the bridge, how can you now be sure, in a fit of anger, that you didn't break her neck?"

"I didn't do it!"

"Was there some reason why you would have wanted Susie McCord dead?"

"No, I didn't kill her!"

"But you're not sure what happened, are you, Randy? Drunk—mad because she resisted your advances— Was that why she ran away?"

"No. I don't know."

"You tried to take advantage of her in the car," Witcher pressed on. "She fought you off and ran away. You caught up to her, ripped off her clothes, hit her hard enough to break her neck, and shoved her into the river. Is that how it was, Randy?"

"I don't know, I— It wasn't that way. I didn't—"

"All we want to hear is the truth, Randy. Just tell us the truth."

"Objection! Badgering!"

Witcher forged ahead. "Is that how it happened, Randy?"

"I didn't do that," Randy cried. "I loved Susie. She was my friend."

Witcher was not impressed. "When you love someone you don't throw her in the river with a broken neck. Tell us what you re-member after that."

"I ran along the river bank looking for her," Randy sobbed. "I knew she couldn't swim, and I wanted to help her."

"You remember doing that? Or are you assuming it because that's what the boys said?"

"I remember doing it."

"Well, now, Randy, you've already told us you didn't remember anything after you chased Susie to the bridge, but now you say you remember looking for her along the river bank. Does that mean you now also recall what took place on the bridge?"

"No, I don't remember."

"You know, Randy, I bet these folks are wondering how in the world you can remember what happened before you got to the bridge. You now recall looking for Susie along the river bank after you fought with her, but you have no recollection of what happened on the bridge. Can you explain that?"

"I don't know. Maybe I freaked out."

"Maybe you freaked out." Witcher's nod was not one of agreement. "Maybe you ripped her clothes off, then maybe you broke her neck because she continued to resist, then maybe you threw her in the river. Was that it, Randy?"

"No! It didn't happen that way."

"How do you know how it happened, if you don't remember?"

"Objection!"

Witcher never broke stride. "Would these young men, Hack and Jason, have any reason not to tell the truth about what they saw that night on the Bois D'Arc River bridge?"

Randy's sullen reply was, "How would I know why a couple of kooks would do anything?"

Witcher's graying head rocked back and forth. His expression told the gathering he was not finished with Randy Marlow. "Why don't you go back to your seat and think about this for a while?"

he said. "Maybe something else will come to mind that we ought to know. Do you want to do that, Randy?"

Randy didn't want to do anything but get out of that chair. He climbed up the bleachers, resuming his seat beside his mother. Jackie grabbed him and held him close.

Witcher called Cecil Combs to the front.

On his way down, Cecil looked at Wiley, seated to his left. Wiley cast him a hang-dog look from the tops of his eyes. Cecil lumbered down the bleachers and took a seat on the chair vacated by Randy.

"Mr. Combs," Witcher said, "I believe you were the one who found the body of Susie McCord in the Bois D'Arc River the morning of September 19, 1954?"

"Me and Wiley was, yes, sir."

"Is that Wiley Hipp you refer to?"

"Yes, sir. Him and me was running our trot lines down below the rapids. Wiley all of a sudden hollered at me, lookee yonder! What's that in the water? Real excited, Wiley was."

"And you investigated?"

"We waded into the water to where Wiley was a-pointin' up agin them boulders, and there she was."

"There who was, Mr. Combs?"

"Why, it was her—Susie. Just a-floatin' around on top of the water. Her eyes was wide open, and her mouth looked like she was hollerin' for help."

Witcher thought for a moment. Neither Randy nor the boys mentioned hearing Susie call out.

"And what did you do then, Mr. Combs?"

"We drug her out, me and Wiley did," Cecil said.

"We seen her neck was broke, and Susie was dead."

"So, your testimony is that when you and Mr. Hipp brought Susie out of the water, she was dead?"

"Yes, sir. 'Bout broke my old heart, it did. I said to Wiley, it just about breaks my old heart for sure."

"And was Susie's body clothed at the time?"

"No, sir, she didn't have no clothes on. I took off my jacket and wrapped it around her 'cause she was all wet and ever'thing."

"And what did you do then?"

"I told Wiley to go on ahead home. I carried Susie up the hill to her mama's place. 'Course, Hilda was all tore up about it."

"Were you friends with the McCord family before this happened?"

"Oh, yes, sir. I knowed Susie's daddy 'fore he died from breathin' all that dust at Mr. Marlow's mill."

"How about Susie? Were you and she close?"

"Like one of my own, Susie was."

Cecil fingered a tear from the corner of his eye. "Just like one of my own."

"Mr. Combs, you've said when you found Susie her mouth was open, like she called for help."

"Yes, sir, it was."

"Yet, if you recall the testimony of Hack and Jason, and Randy Marlow, neither of them heard Susie call out. Why do you suppose that was?"

"I—I—I reckon I don't know why that was, sir. Her mouth was open like she—" His voice trailed off.

Witcher nodded, pondering the old man's statement. "Mr. Combs, how do you think Susie got into the water, and wound up on those rocks?"

Cecil gave his head a bewildered shake. "I ain't got no idy. 'Course they's been talk about the Marlow boy havin' something to do with it."

"Objection!" Barrickman screamed. "Hearsay! It has not been established that Mr. Randy Marlow had anything to do with the death of Susie McCord."

Witcher said, "Mr. Combs, do you know Randy Marlow?"

"If your name is Marlow," Cecil said, "it ain't easy to hide it in this town."

"I understand you worked in the mills for Mr. Amos Marlow?"

"Yes, sir. Forty-two year. I give it up four year ago."

"And you would have no reason to doubt the character of his grandson, would you?"

"I reckon not."

Witcher thanked him. Cecil went back to his seat with a strong look at Wiley. Wiley looked the other way.

Witcher said, "The next name on my list is that of Marshal Chink Petty."

Petty cleared his throat and stirred in his seat beside Amos. Chink cast Barrickman a questioning glance. Barrickman gave him an "I can't help you" look.

"However, Marshal," Witcher said, "if you don't mind, I'd like to ask Mr. Wiley Hipp to come forward at this time."

Chink relaxed, relief melting into his cowboy boots.

Hipp, hollow-eyed and slump-shouldered, slouched down the bleachers and dropped into the wit-ness chair.

"Mr. Hipp," Witcher said. "You're a friend to Cecil Combs?"

"Yes, sir, I am. Best friend a feller ever had, Cecil is."

"And the two of you were together when you found the body of Susie McCord?"

"Yes, sir, we was."

"Can you tell us how that came about?"

"Yes, sir, I can."

Wiley glanced at Cecil. Cecil nodded his head as if to instruct the little guy.

To Witcher, Wiley said, "Can I say something else first?"

"Go ahead."

"Mr. Marlow's been awful good to me," Wiley said. "After I come home from the war, jobs was hard to come by. Mr. Marlow put me to work in the lumber mill, and I been there ever since. He paid a bill or two I didn't have money for, like he done for lots of other people, I'd guess.

"Now, I know he's been in a stew about Susie dyin', 'cause he's not for sure whether Randy was the one that done it or not. I seen Randy grow up. He wasn't no model kid, I'll give you that. I tried a time or two to spark his mama, but she wouldn't have nothin' to do with me."

The gallery chuckled.

"It looked like there wasn't gonna be no trial or nothin'," Wiley continued, "and I figgered I was better off keepin' my mouth shut. Now, that guy in the red car comes around askin' questions like he's hellbent to get to the bottom of it, and— Well, it might not come to nothin', but I gotta tell you what I seen that night."

"What did you see, Mr. Hipp?" Witcher said.

"It got to be midnight, and Cecil told me to go on home, and he'd finish runnin' the lines."

"How did you know it was midnight?"

"I heard that music and the clock was strikin'."

"Because it was late on a Saturday night, Mr. Combs told you to go on home?"

"Yes, sir, he did."

"And he was going to finish running the trot lines?"

"Yes, sir."

"So, you went on home like Mr. Combs told you, and left Cecil alone to run the trot lines?"

"Yes, sir, I did.

"All right. What happened after that?"

"I didn't get downstream very far till I heard some kind of commotion going on behind me, back where I left Cecil. Like them boys said, the moon was real bright. I jerked my head around and seen Cecil wadin' into the river. At first I thought somebody was pullin' a prank on him, but then I seen him draggin' somethin' up out of the water. I took a minute to think about if maybe I oughta go back and help. Then I seen Cecil scufflin' with somebody, and I heard a scream that sounded like a girl, and it was. She was kickin' and squirmin' like she was tryin' to get loose, then I never heard her scream no more."

Cecil struggled to his feet, and shouted, "You

drunk bastard, quit your lyin'!"

"I ain't lyin', Cece. I told you I never forgot nothin'."

"Like hell you ain't!"

To Witcher, Hipp said, "When I seen Cecil throw her back in the water, I didn't know what to do. I couldn't tell who it was he th'owed back, o' course, but I never woulda believed it was Susie. Cecil was my friend, and I never figgered he'd hurt nobody on purpose. So, I just went on home, like he told me to. The next mornin', him and me drug Susie's body out of the river, like he said."

The crowd waited in shocked silence.

"Mr. Hipp," Witcher said, "are you saying Cecil Combs killed Susie McCord?"

"I ain't sayin' nothin' like that. All I'm sayin' is what I seen."

Cecil made a feeble effort to get to Wiley, but someone grabbed him and pulled him back into his seat.

Witcher said, "Mr. Combs, your friend Wiley Hipp has described a scene that makes it look like you were responsible for the death of Susie McCord. What have you to say to that?"

The crowd was aghast. All eyes were locked on the old fat man they pitied, suffering with him, re-calling how he labored up the hill bearing Susie's lifeless body to her mother's front door. Now, he was exposed as the one who killed the girl whose body he carried.

Pale as milk, bushy gray head bowed, Cecil's crinkled old eyes were fixed on his beefy hands, grip-ping each other between his knees.

"Mr. Combs?" Witcher said.

"She was all wet and cold," Cecil whispered. "I didn't go to hurt her. She wouldn't stop screamin' at me. All I wanted was to get them wet clothes off of her, and make her warm. Just like Ruthie. It was just like I was draggin' Ruthie out of the river." He shook his head sadly. "Like one of my own, Susie was. Just like one of my own."

"What about her clothes, Mr. Combs? Do you know what became of them?"

"Why, I took 'em home," Cecil said simply. "That's where they belonged—at my house."

Witcher surveyed the stunned crowd to see if anyone had further comments or questions. There were none.

He pounded the gavel. "This meeting is over," he said. "Marshal Petty."

Chink moved toward Cecil.

Witcher folded up his briefcase and took off for the exit. From behind him he heard someone blurt his name. He turned on a heel and looked into the rage-red face of Amos Marlow.

"You put that boy through hell!" Amos shouted. "After all I've done for you!"

"Well, Amos, what you have done for me," Witcher said, "is help me remember who I am."

"You'll live to regret this!"

"I wouldn't be surprised." Witcher took a look around to see if anyone else was within earshot. "You know, Amos, the next time you try to bribe somebody, you'd better be sure you can trust him to keep his mouth shut." Witcher took another glance at the milling crowd. They didn't hear what they hoped to hear but, thanks to the persistence of an out-of-work newsman named Timberlake, they no longer had to guess who killed Susie McCord.

"I believed Randy's story," Witcher said to Amos. "But if I hadn't been tough on him, Hipp might not have remembered what you did for him, and betrayed his friend Combs." He tucked his briefcase under an arm. "There comes a time when we all have to be reminded of who we are. You and I both have some soul-searching to do. Goodbye, Amos."

Witcher extended his hand, but Amos ignored it, and limped away to join Randy and Jackie on their way out. He responded with a sad smile then traded nods with Timberlake as he strode toward the exit.

A surge of outraged humanity spewed its wrath upon the old fat man. Cecil wrapped his arms around his head to protect himself from angry blows. Three men laid hold of him and started hauling him down from the bleachers. Jeff joined Chink, to rescue Cecil from the onslaught. They pushed their way through the mob dragging Cecil across the gym floor. Chink and Jeff tossed aside a few bodies, then grabbed the old man's arms and wrenched him free, battered and bleeding.

A heavyset, raw-boned man kicked at Cecil and scowled at Chink. "Give it up, Buster," Chink said to him. "There's been trouble enough."

Buster Mills, red-faced and out for blood, looked for support from his cronies lined up on his side.

Chink knew Buster's crew didn't care about seeing justice done. Nor were they concerned about what Cecil did. They were a part of the crowd, unleashing their hostility for being denied the truth for four years.

"We could jump you and take him," Buster sneered at Chink.

Chink eased his hands to his waist, right hand hovering near the gun on his hip.

"It ain't over yet," Mills said with a lame threat.

"It had better be over," Chink said, "or you won't like what happens next."

Buster backed off with a scowl, and took his friends with him.

Chink and Jeff each grabbed an arm and steered Cecil toward the exit.

With a simple grin, Cecil said, "It looks like somebody's finally gonna pay for that, don't it, Chink?"

"It looks like, Cecil."

"Yes, sir, somebody's finally gonna pay for that."

Cecil glanced over his shoulder. Wiley was moping a couple of steps to his right.

"Bye, Wiley," Cecil said. "Be seein' you."

"You hadn't oughta called me that, Cecil!" Wiley wailed. "You shouldna called me no drunk stupid bastard!" His shoulders shook. He hid his face in his hands.

Jackie caught Jeff's eye, cast him a thank you smile, and walked away with an arm around Randy. Randy shrugged as if it was no big deal.

Jeff acknowledged Jackie's nod and moved on.

Amos limped along behind Randy and Jackie, tugging at his goatee.

Chink took charge of Cecil and led him away.

Jeff said, "Do you need help getting him out of here?"

With a toss of his head, Chink let him know he had everything under control.

Now it can be Told

Mason Bryer practically sprinted back to his office. He couldn't wait to get in front of that old Remington and start pecking out the saga of Susie McCord.

Mason's yellow notepad was full of notes, and he knew exactly how he was going to write the story of Susie McCord. He'd start with the headline: MARLOW KID CLEARED, OLD CODGER NAILED! What pathos, what tragedy, what drama! The story would write itself. But it would have to wait.

Sally Hargis met him at the door, holding out to him a small pink envelope. The look in her eyes told him it was no ordinary envelope.

Slowly Mason turned it over, checking the postmark, as he checked every postmark on every envelope for four years. This one was from Whittier, California. Mason's heart began racing at an unusual pace. He went into his office and closed the door. Eager as he was to learn its contents, he hesitated to open it, afraid of what he might find inside. Someone must have died, or at least met with a serious accident, or maybe contracted some life threatening illness.

Carefully he slit the seal and removed the sheet of pink stationery was folded in half.

"Dear dad," his teary eyes read, "can you come home for Christmas? The kids are anxious to see their granddad. So am I."

There was more, but his misty eyes swept to the bottom of the page, looking for the signature he knew would be there.

"I love you, dad. Rita."

Sally's eyes could have bored holes in Mason's closed door.

When the door finally opened, filled with his bulk, a shiver of delight rippled through her body. Never before had she seen in his eyes what she now saw. A look of pleading. Sort of loving, as Mason was capable of showing love.

"Sally," he said with the tenderness that for years she dreamed of one day hearing. "Can you come in for a minute?"

Flushed with the thrill of anticipation, across her mind raced the countless late nights she and Mason spent creating an ad layout, reworking a story that didn't quite come off, wrapping up loose ends, putting the paper to bed. Flooding back were the many hours of being close to him, peering over his shoulder, weakened by the closeness of his massive body. How she ached to be crushed in his arms, willing that he succumb to the magnetism of the perfume for which she paid half a week's salary.

Maybe now. Maybe—

On legs of rubber she reached his door. "Yes, Mr. Bryer?"

"Come in, Sally," Mason said, "and close the door."

Gently he took her hand and drew her to him.

"Oh, Mr. Bryer!"
"Call me Mason."

The Discovery of Zack Wheeler

In the Marlow cemetery, Jeff knelt beside the grave he and Amy knew they'd find there. "Did you bring the flowers?" he asked.

Amy handed him the glass vase filled with daisies, and he placed it beside the headstone.

Susie McCord
Feb. 17, 1937–Sept. 18, 1954
Now she rests.

Amy said, "I found something else you'll want to see."

Jeff spent another silent moment paying tribute to the young girl he never knew, but whose death changed his life. Amy took his hand and led him to the next aisle over. She pointed to a headstone almost hidden by grass and weeds. Jeff heaved a deep sigh, giving his head a relieved shake.

Finally, he found Zack Wheeler.

Capt. Zachary Louis Wheeler, U. S. Army
March 1, 1910—June 6, 1944
He gave his life for his country.

The mysterious Zachary Wheeler, Jeff thought. *At last we meet.* "Who are you?" he whispered.

The response was as silent as the time-and-weather rusted stone that marked his grave.

So, this was how it was to end, his search for Zachary Wheeler, and his search for the truth of how the life of Susie McCord came to an end, fewer than fifty feet apart.

Jeff wasn't ready to leave. Amy slipped a hand into his and led him to the red Corvette. He slid under the wheel, turned the key, and pulled down the visor against the setting sun. His mother's white envelope dropped onto his lap. He picked it up, studied it for a moment. He flipped open the glove compartment, and started to place the envelope inside.

"Aren't you going to read it?" Amy said.

"It's not my letter."

"You're not afraid to open it, are you?"

"Afraid? Of course not. Why would I be afraid?"

"Why don't you open it?"

"It's addressed to Zachary Wheeler."

"Well, it's too late for him. Do you want me to open it?"

"Whose letter is this anyway?"

"You are afraid, aren't you?"

Jeff took a deep breath, cast Amy a tolerant look. He ripped open the envelope and began reading.

"My darling Zachary,

"April 12, 1926 was the most memorable day of my life. I'm so glad you were there when I closed the dress shop and asked if you could drive me home on a rainy night. I had not the remotest thought of asking you in until the moment it happened.

"You must have thought me some kind of brazen

hussy to be so bold, but I'm happy I did! You left me with a precious gift that I have cherished for the rest of my life, which is now ending. So often I felt lonely and unneeded when Ethan was away, but I have always been glad he was gone this time!

"Time and circumstance kept us apart for these many years. The few letters we were able to exchange softened my longing for you, but nothing could fill the void left by your absence. When at last I became resigned to life without you—though I waited endlessly for your return, pretending you were away in the war, as well you might have been—every time I held my son in my arms, cuddling him, caring for him, I relived the thrill of our brief time together, trusting that your memory was as strong as mine is still.

"I pray that this letter reaches you, and finds you well, so you will know that the one who brings it is our son Jeff.

"I regret not sharing this with you long ago. Please, forgive me.

Love always, Leota."

A Moment of Passion

Zachary helped her into his car that rainy night. The moment their hands touched, through Leota's body surged a magical sensation she never felt with Ethan. Shocked by her impulsive desire to invite Zachary into her home for a cup of coffee, Leota emitted a nervous giggle, giddy as a teenager.

"I don't know," Zachary said. "With your man gone—"

"It's all right," Leota assured him. "If Ethan were here, he'd invite you himself."

One cup of coffee became two, then three. As the evening grew into night, Leota brought from the kitchen pantry a bottle of cherry wine Ethan reserved for "purposes of purification."

Ethan never invited her to share it.

Long past midnight, Zachary left her languishing in the afterglow of sheer ecstasy, her cheeks aflame with the heat of passion. Her body trembled with the release of emotions that for years smoldered beneath layers of pretended contentment, awaiting their time to erupt. Neither guilt nor shame did she suffer. Nor did she seek forgiveness for conceiving in a moment of boundless joy the son who was her only happiness. Steeling herself against the fanatical demands of life with the pious Ethan, she often stole away to a private reverie where sadness found no place, basking once more in her secret thrill, finding fulfillment again in her memories of Zachary Wheeler. Whether he was alive or dead she didn't know, but she was driven to write the letter, hoping somehow it would find its way into the hands of the man she loved once only, but whose gift lasted a lifetime.

Amy gave Jeff a moment to absorb what he read.

"Are you surprised," she said.

"Surprised?"

"About your mother and Zachary."

"Yes, but I must admit I have wondered about that."

She touched his hand.

"How does it feel," she said, "knowing the man

you lived with most of your life was not your father?"

"I haven't had time to think about that."

"Are you sorry?"

Jeff was in no mood to talk about it, but Amy's question deserved an answer.

"I'm sorry for my mother," he said, "not for myself. All those years she suffered with Ethan—"

She squeezed his hand.

"Ethan used to tell me I'd never amount to a nosebleed in a slaughter house." He glanced at Amy with half a smile. "I've spent a lot of time proving him right."

"You're a good man, Jeff Timberlake."

"You know what's funny?" he said. "I wish my father had been my dad."

"There's nothing funny about that." She kissed him on the cheek. "Let's go."

In his rearview mirror Jeff saw the flashing lights of the trailing Ford Fairlane. He pulled to the curb and stopped, breathed a deep, tolerant sigh, and said to Amy, "Well, I guess the law never sleeps, does it?"

Chink Petty pulled over and parked behind the Corvette. He took a leisurely stroll from the cruiser to Jeff's side of the red car. He leaned in, and nodded to Amy.

"Have I done something wrong, officer?" Jeff said.

"I don't know yet," Chink said. "Maybe we need to talk about that."

With a wink at Amy, he said, "What's it like cruising around town in a fancy red car with a big time hero?"

"Aaah, come on, Chink," Jeff said.

"You know I was wrong about you," the marshal said.

"Everybody is entitled to one mistake."

"Uh-huh. We might never have known the truth about Susie if you hadn't happened by. Nobody else had the courage to stay with it and see how it played out."

"Okay."

"I want you to know I took care of that Pretty Boy thing," Chink said. "I should have locked him up, and I may yet." To Amy, he said, "I thought you'd like to know that Jackie is arranging some psycho tests for her dad."

"Oh? How is Jackie?"

"She's okay. Relieved that it's over. She worried about Amos. My guess is she'll keep Randy around for a while till they find out something about her dad, then he'll be going back to school."

"And where does Chink Petty go from here?" Jeff said.

"Well, I've heard some talk about an election for town marshal."

"You're the town marshal," Jeff said.

"I was never elected, you know. I was sort of appointed."

"Why would anybody run against you?"

Chink grinned. "I hope it ain't you."

"No way," Jeff said. "I'm outta here." He shifted the Corvette into gear. "What's going to happen to Cecil?" Jeff asked.

"I've got him in my jail. What happens next is

up to Witcher and the court."

To Amy, Petty said, "Are you gonna be gone forever?"

"Oh, no. I do have a job, you know."

"She'll be back," Jeff said, "and I may be with her."

"You'll be welcome."

"Red car and all?"

"Red car and all."

Chink stuck out his hand, and Jeff shook it. "Tell Dottie to keep that griddle warm," Jeff said.

The marshal gave them a two-finger salute and watched the red Corvette grow small as it headed north, turning east toward St. Louis.

Petty climbed into his cruiser with its lights flashing and siren blaring wide open. He split Main Street at pursuit speed, reminding the city of Marlow who was in charge.

Maybe now, he told himself with a satisfied smile, he had grown up to be the man Zelda thought she married.

The City Hall clock struck four.

Where is Hale Witcher?

The October 13th edition of the Lansburg Press proclaimed: "Mrs. Essie Witcher, socialite and philanthropist, of one of the city's most prominent families, was granted a divorce from her husband of twenty-six years, County Attorney Hale Witcher."

On the Society Page of the same edition appeared an item that stated, "Donna Jean (Mrs. Bruce) Caster will be out of the city for an extended visit with friends in New Orleans."

October sixteenth, the Press reported the disappearance of "County Attorney Hale Witcher, "—absent from his office, not seen by friends nor business associates for more than three days.

Witcher is listed as missing by Sheriff Clay Mitchell. Mitchell says Witcher informed no one of his whereabouts, and left no directives with his office. Mitchell promises a thorough investigation.

The sheriff would not comment on whether foul play was suspected in the disappearance of the popular county attorney.

Two days later a fisherman named Lance Keeny called Mitchell's office and said his bass boat scraped the top of a car submerged in the Bois D'Arc River half way between Lansburg and Marlow. Mitchell had a crew out there before noon, pulling that car out of the river. The sheriff, a short, square man of fifty-two, directed the operation from the river bank.

A diver surfaced, and yelled, "We got it, Sheriff!"

"Is anybody in there?" Mitchell called.

"Somebody's in there!"

A dozen people, Chink Petty and Mason Bryer among them, gathered to witness the operation. All eyes focused on the spot where the diver emerged, curious as to what the car might yield once it was hauled onto the bank.

A truck backed up to the edge of the river, and reeled a length of cable into the water. The diver grabbed the cable and secured it to the car's rear bumper.

To the winch operator, Mitchell said, "Okay, Lucky, bring her out!"

Lucky Braun threw a lever and the winch turned. The cable came taut and stiffened. The truck's rear wheels began to sink into the muddy bank, then caught and held. Slowly the winch reeled in the cable.

"Keep coming," Mitchell said. "You're doing fine."

The rear end of the car broke the surface of the water, revealing its pale blue color. A moment later the car was identified as a bird egg blue 1956 Lincoln Continental.

Somebody said in a half whisper, "That's Witcher's car!"

Mitchell shouted, "Get that sucker out of there!"

Braun threw another lever, locking the winch in place, inching the car up out of the water with a taut cable. Slowly the rear end of the Continental crept up the bank.

When half the car cleared the river, Mitchell leaped into the waist-deep water and peered inside.

"Petty! Bryer!" he yelled. "You want to come down here?"

The two splashed into the water, and Mitchell stood aside while they took a look.

"Damn, Clay!" Chink said. "That's Hale Witcher!"

Bryer said, "Who's the woman?"

"Donna Jean Caster."

***

In November, Blake Baldwin was re-elected to Congress for a third term, and Chink Petty was voted without opposition to the office of police chief in the City of Marlow.

In December, Jackie formed her own band and took it on the road, realizing her dream of becoming a professional country singer. The following Spring Jackie signed a contract with RCA Victor Records. Ten months later she had three releases in Billboard's Top 50.

Randy graduated from the University of Missouri, and became his mother's road manager.

* * *

In the psychiatric ward of the Osage County Hospital, Amos Marlow underwent a series of tests and was released after three weeks. He was diagnosed with nothing more serious than "intermittent paranoia," for which he declined treatment.

During his stay at the hospital, Amos challenged fellow patient Cecil Combs to checker games at a picnic table under the elms on the hospital grounds. Amos always won.

Extensive testing proved Cecil incompetent to stand trial for the murder of Susie McCord. He was committed to the state hospital for the mentally ill where he died in 1967.

He was seventy-six years old.

In nine years, Cecil's only visitor was Wiley Hipp who, every Monday morning, brought his old friend a pot of steaming chili.

***

For thirteen months Jeff served on the news staff of Radio Station KMOX in St. Louis. At the behest of Charlene Gore, he left KMOX and became the St. Louis bureau chief for National News Service

Amy's last year at Marlow High was 1958-59. She moved to St. Louis, became Mrs. Jeff Timberlake, and taught for two more years in St. Louis public schools.

Upon the arrival of Zachary, the first of two sons, Amy gave up teaching, and became a full time stay-at-home mom. At last report, the Timberlakes were living happy ever after in their rambling ranch style home in Chesterfield, Missouri.

Jeff and Amy often reflected with sadness on what had brought them together. Still, they could not deny their good fortune of having found each other because of a young dead girl named Susie McCord.

ABOUT THE AUTHOR

An accomplished author with many books to his credit, David A. Estes draws on his wide experience, from the cotton fields of Oklahoma and Texas where he grew up, to the islands of the South Pacific where he served as a United States Marine, to the market place in America where he retired from a career in broadcasting.

David writes westerns and mysteries, along with many other genres of novels and short stories. He lives on his family farm in West Central Missouri with two black Labs and a suspicious cat.

OTHER PUBLICATIONS

Available at amazon.com, barnsandnoble.com, abebooks.com and more

Angel on My Back
Wet Dogs Don't Ride
Blood on the Wall
A Bag of Gold

Coming Soon:
Ajax and Elbow Grease
Big Boy

www.ingramcontent.com/pod-product-compliance
Lightning Source LLC
Chambersburg PA
CBHW061141170626
46809CB00003B/945